Lucas and Valerie's U
Surprise Parenthood:

1. Be certain "Daddy" knows that a toddler will not fit into a diaper meant for a newborn—no matter what he tries.

2. Never turn your back for a second. Your kids will let you know why.

3. If you want a little private time with your spouse, you should have thought of it *before* the stork arrived. For ultimate snuggle time, set your alarm clock ahead an hour—or two, or three....

4. Always have a list of emergency numbers nearby: fire, police, poison control...and most important—the baby-sitter!

5. Keep in mind, between food fights and 2:00 a.m. screaming fits, that happiness will be your reward. (That, and the fact that your children will eventually have kids of their own.)

Dear Reader,

Whether or not it's back to school—for you *or* the kids—Special Edition this month is the place to return to for romance!

Our THAT SPECIAL WOMAN!, Serena Fanon, is heading straight for a Montana wedding in Jackie Merritt's *Montana Passion,* the second title in Jackie's MADE IN MONTANA miniseries. But that's not the only wedding this month—in Christine Flynn's *The Black Sheep's Bride,* another blushing bride joins the family in the latest installment of THE WHITAKER BRIDES. And three little matchmakers scheme to bring their unsuspecting parents back together again in *Daddy of the House,* book one of Diana Whitney's new miniseries, PARENTHOOD.

This month, the special cross-line miniseries DADDY KNOWS LAST comes to Special Edition. In *Married... With Twins!,* Jennifer Mikels tells the tale of a couple on the brink of a breakup—that is, until they become instant parents to two adorable girls. September brings two Silhouette authors to the Special Edition family for the first time. Shirley Larson's *A Cowboy Is Forever* is a reunion ranch story not to be missed, and in Ingrid Weaver's latest, *The Wolf and the Woman's Touch,* a sexy loner agrees to help a woman find her missing niece—but only if she'll give him one night of passion.

I hope you enjoy each and every story to come!

Sincerely,

Tara Gavin,
Senior Editor

Please address questions and book requests to:
Silhouette Reader Service
U.S.: 3010 Walden Ave., P.O. Box 1325, Buffalo, NY 14269
Canadian: P.O. Box 609, Fort Erie, Ont. L2A 5X3

JENNIFER MIKELS

Married...With Twins!

Silhouette ®

SPECIAL ◆ EDITION ®

Published by Silhouette Books
America's Publisher of Contemporary Romance

This one is for Jessica O'Kelley and Joan Cottrell,
with many thanks.

Special thanks and acknowledgment to Jennifer Mikels
for her contribution to the Daddy Knows Last series.

 SILHOUETTE BOOKS

ISBN 0-373-24054-6

MARRIED...WITH TWINS!

Copyright © 1996 by Harlequin Books S.A.

Printed in U.S.A.

JENNIFER MIKELS

started out an avid fan of historical novels, which eventually led her to contemporary romances, which in turn led her to try her hand at penning her own novels. She quickly found she preferred romance fiction with its happy endings to the technical writing she'd done for a public-relations firm. Between writing and raising two boys, the Phoenix-based author has little time left for hobbies, though she does enjoy cross-country skiing and antique shopping with her husband.

Meet The Soon-To-Be Moms
of New Hope, Texas!

"I'll do anything to have a baby—even if it means
going to the sperm bank. Unless sexy cowboy
Jake Spencer is willing to be a daddy...
the natural way."
—*Priscilla Barrington, hopeful mom-to-be.*

THE BABY NOTION
by Dixie Browning (Desire 7/96)

"I'm more than willing to help Mitch McCord take care
of the baby he found on his doorstep. After all, I've been
in love with that confirmed bachelor for years."
—*Jenny Stevens, maternal girl-next-door.*

BABY IN A BASKET
by Helen R. Myers (Romance 8/96)

"My soon-to-be ex-husband and I are soon-to-be
parents! Can our new arrivals also bless us with a
second chance at marriage?"
—*Valerie Kincaid, married new mom.*

MARRIED...WITH TWINS!
by Jennifer Mikels (Special Edition 9/96)

"I have vowed to be married by the time I turn thirty.
But the only man who interests me is single dad
Travis Donovan—and he doesn't know I'm alive...yet!"
—*Wendy Wilcox,
biological-clock-counting bachelorette.*

HOW TO HOOK A HUSBAND (AND A BABY)
by Carolyn Zane (Yours Truly 10/96)

"Everybody wants me to name the father of my baby.
But I can't tell anyone—even the expectant daddy!"
—*Faith Harper, prim, proper—and very pregnant.*

DISCOVERED: DADDY
by Marilyn Pappano (Intimate Moments 11/96)

Chapter One

"You're a daddy now," someone had said to him. He couldn't even remember who'd said the words. He'd been reeling from the shock. Unlike other men who had nine months to prepare for fatherhood, Lucas Kincaid had become a daddy overnight.

Fate threw some real curves, he decided, dropping the tailgate on the borrowed truck he'd parked in his driveway. Just as he and his wife were on the verge of divorce, they'd become the guardians of twin two-year-olds.

Disbelief still shadowing him, he cradled a Victorian dollhouse in his arms and turned toward the back door of the split-level house that he and Val had bought four years ago.

From the kitchen, ear-piercing screams drifted to him.

"Sounds as if Valerie has her hands full, Lucas," a neighbor yelled out with a wave.

A sun that promised another warm September day glared in his eyes as he squinted at Kate Whitton ambling toward him.

"Those twins are sure adorable-looking," she said in her strong Texas drawl.

Luke thought so, too. Urchins with blond ponytails, pug noses and quick grins, Brooke and Traci Dawson had kept Val and him on their toes since seven this morning. And more than once had given them an indication of life with toddlers in the terrible two stage.

"If you need help, let us know." Kate gestured toward the truck that was loaded with toys and cartons. "They certainly have a lot."

Luke merely nodded. For six years, Carrie Dawson had longed for pregnancy. When she'd learned she was expecting, she and Joe had been elated at the news that she was carrying twins.

"I'll stop in later and see if Valerie wants help."

To tell Kate no would have caused more of a problem. Luke sidestepped two tricycles and nearly kicked over Val's clay pot filled with geraniums. He'd always wanted children. He knew a lot of men could care less, but of all the patients he saw, he liked the kids best. They asked the most absurd questions, they lightened his day, they made him remember why he'd decided on a career in medicine.

After medical school, he'd returned to New Hope, the town he'd been born and raised in, and had opened his practice because he liked personal one-on-one contact with patients. Some viewed him as a confidant, like Agnes, who had an allergy to penicillin and a tough time with widowhood. Some had become relatives, like Edwin, Val's crusty-mannered grandfather. Others had developed into good friends, the best, like Joe and Carrie Dawson.

Nearing the back door, he shifted the dollhouse to one arm and reached to open the screen door. A soft breeze fluttered around him as he paused and peered over the top of the dollhouse.

His gaze went to his wife. A small, slender woman with long legs and hair the color of deep, rich coffee, she had the lithe figure of an athlete or a dancer. Her dark brown eyes were wide and expressive, her face animated as she talked low to the twins. In her hand was the object of the battle, a Raggedy Ann doll.

Pouting two-year-olds glared up at her until she stretched and grabbed two cookies from an opened package on the counter.

Traci's pout lifted first. She crawled onto Val's lap and curled an arm around her neck. More interested in the cookie than affection, Brooke plopped on the floor to munch away.

"Cookie." Traci waved it, then scrambled off Val's lap.

At the slam of the screen door behind him, Val angled a look over her shoulder in his direction. Out of necessity, they'd spent more time together this morning than they had in weeks. "Where is this going?" he asked about the dollhouse.

"Good question," she said, actually sounding a little amused. She paused in unpacking a carton overflowing with stuffed animals and dolls, and unconsciously raked fingers through her short-cropped hairstyle. It was a familiar gesture, one he'd seen often when she'd been in his office hunched over the ledgers or seated at the reception desk, greeting patients. "Your den," she finally answered, and shrugged.

That wasn't the response he'd expected, but he didn't protest. Though she was usually organized, she looked a bit overwhelmed. Luke sensed she had no idea where to put anything except the twins' clothes.

"Hi, lion," Brooke sang out as Val lifted a fuzzy tan animal from the carton of stuffed animals. All morning she'd greeted everything that had been unpacked. As Lucas inched his way around her, her blond head swiveled toward him. "Lu-cas, don't drop."

Amusement rippled through him. He'd had his share of toddlers in his office, but their tendency toward bossiness had eluded him until this up-close and personal encounter. Crossing the living room, he felt resistance on his leg.

"Can me help?" Brooke asked, still yanking on his jeans.

Traci suddenly tugged on the other leg. "No." Her blond ponytail swung with the wag of her head. "Traci help Luke."

As Brooke's fingers tightened on the denim, Luke contemplated another battle. It took no effort to envision each twin grabbing at the dollhouse until it fell from his arms. Only one possibility existed after that. Tears and wails. Holding the dollhouse above their reaching hands, he braced his backside against the short banister of the stairway that led to the second level of the house, and patiently he waited.

Never more than a step behind the girls, Val predictably popped around the kitchen doorway, her arms hugging stuffed animals.

Was it good-humored sympathy or something else he read in the dark gaze smiling at him?

"Me help," Brooke insisted, her little hand grabbing at the bottom of the dollhouse.

Luke had seen his wife cool tempers during city council meetings, soothe her sometimes cantankerous grandfather, and quiet patients in the waiting room outside his office who were stressing over medical tests. She possessed a soft voice and the ability to say the right thing at the appropriate time. He hoped that was all true at this moment.

Letting the stuffed animals tumble from her arms onto the living room carpet, she flashed a quick, amused smile. It tore at him. For months he'd yearned to see her like this. Instead sorrow had haunted her eyes. "Girls, I need help," she said, offering a hand to each twin.

With no hesitation, Brooke bounded to her. "Me do it."

Just as eager, Traci trailed. "Traci do it."

"Round three," Luke said on a chuckle.

Val looked his way. For an instant she could almost remember the way they used to be. As he headed for the den, she urged the girls into the kitchen. "Both of you can help." It took a second of quick thinking to find a job for them. After dumping plastic containers onto the floor with instructions to choose three, she sent them toward the sandbox in the backyard.

While Traci perched on the edge of the tractor tire, Brooke sat inside it, the plastic containers and plastic garden tools strewn across the grass.

Surprisingly the transition from the home the girls had always known to a new one hadn't been as difficult as Val had expected. She assumed that was because the twins were comfortable with her and Luke. As godparents, they'd baby-sat often. They'd been there for every birthday and every holiday.

Turning away from the door, she flicked on the radio before settling on a stool at the breakfast bar to sort through a bag of clothing. Slowly, she lifted a pair of pink tights from it. She still couldn't believe Joe and Carrie were dead, their fate sealed by a drunk driver. Why? Why them? she wondered.

Sadness flowed through her for a woman she'd thought of like a sister, for a man who'd been her husband's boyhood friend, for all they would miss with their daughters.

At the shuffle of Luke's sneakers behind her, Val nudged herself from dark thoughts. It did no good to linger over what had happened during the past few weeks. All that mattered now were the twins.

"Where did the dynamic duo disappear to?" he asked.

"They're in the backyard. They love the sandbox," she said, wanting him to know his efforts were being appreciated. Yesterday he'd moved the tractor tire from Joe and Carrie's backyard while the twins had been napping. After a trip to the building materials store, he'd filled the tire with a fresh supply of sand. "I'm sure finding it here is helping them adjust,'' she added because he'd wandered for a second to the French door as if to see for himself.

With a brush at her bangs, Val watched him leave. Who are you? she wondered. When they'd met, she'd thought he was the perfect one for her. With his tall, rangy build, dark hair, chiseled features and deep-set, blue eyes, he'd garnered his share of ogling women, but her feelings had gone beyond his good looks. Personable and intelligent, he'd been easy to talk to, easy to laugh with, and wonderful to make love with.

Then, on a February night, their world had screeched to a halt. There had been months since that night when they couldn't be around each other, couldn't stand to see each other's eyes and the sadness that mirrored their own. She'd withdrawn within herself. He'd drifted away from her, spending more time at his office, volunteering for more night duty in the emergency room of the hospital, growing more silent. They'd stopped talking and laughing. They'd stopped making love. And they'd faced the inevitable weeks ago. Their marriage was over.

She doubted she'd ever feel comfortable with what she viewed as failure. Looking toward the window, she saw Luke heft the mattresses for the twins' cribs above his head and, balancing them on it, start for the back door. He wouldn't ask her for help, but she'd offer it anyway. She met him at the door and opened it. ''We could have asked some friends over to unload the truck.''

''Jake volunteered,'' he answered. ''So did Mitch.''

Why he'd refused wasn't difficult to understand. If they'd been around, they might have sensed something was wrong between Luke and her. Val stepped aside, her hands raising to offer support if he needed it. Fielding friends' concerned questions had obviously bothered him more than a couple of hours sweating and straining muscles.

As he maneuvered the mattresses past her, Val glanced at the clock. She spent a few moments gathering fixings for lunch before she called the girls. While she swiped peanut butter and jelly across slices of bread, then dished out peaches, they sat at their miniature table, talking to their dolls and filling cups with imaginary tea. Did they like peaches? she wondered. Or should she give them bananas? Nothing was simple. She wanted so badly to give them as much normalcy as possible. And she felt so inept.

"That's all of it except a few cartons," Luke said, propping two high chairs against the wall.

Val wished she could tell him how filled with doubts she was. She wished she could ask him about something as unimportant as what fruit to serve, because everything seemed significant to her now.

"Where are you going to put all of the stuff from their playroom?" Unexpectedly he stopped beside her and snatched one of the carrot sticks she'd sliced seconds ago.

As casual as he was, she felt tense with him standing so close. "In here and the dining room—for now." Val scowled at her prepared lunch. Insecurities rising again, she spoke low to him. "Do you think they like peaches?"

It was impossible for him not to hear the shadow of concern in her voice. "Peaches—yeah. They like peaches," he answered as he sensed she was looking for an assurance. Her uncertainty surprised him. She was a strong woman with a mind of her own. "Don't you remember? Carrie had a thing for peach ice cream, and the twins always helped her eat it."

"Yes." She said the word on a sigh. "Why didn't I remember that?"

He thought the answer to her question was obvious. "Probably because there's so much else to think about."

Like us, Val mused, listening to the squeak of the screen door closing behind him.

While the twins ate, she swept a look over the mess in the large country kitchen. It was going to take longer than she'd thought to get them settled in. She'd make some headway today. She had to, or the disorder would drive her crazy. Even when she and Luke had bought the house, she'd been unrelenting about getting everything in order. He'd laughed at her, and he'd distracted her, she recalled. He'd seduced her in this kitchen. They'd laughed. They'd dreamed of the family they'd raise in this house. And, she reminded herself quickly, they'd also discussed divorce in this same room.

"Done," Brooke announced, grabbing Val's attention.

With some satisfaction, she noted they'd eaten all of their lunch. After wiping hands and faces, she ushered them outside. As if it were Christmas, they tore at the brown bags she handed them.

"Bub-bles," Brooke squealed.

Leaving the back door open to hear a dispute, Val left them alone gleefully blowing, then chasing, bubbles.

More bags of clothes demanded her attention. She tossed a few worn tops and pants into a garbage bag, then quickly retrieved each one, worried she was throwing away a favorite.

"The cribs are set up in the bedroom," Luke announced behind her.

She swiveled a look back to see him retrieving the ice tea pitcher from the refrigerator. Though the twins' pink-and-white dollhouse hardly belonged in his den, a masculine room of leather and tweed, she believed that the upstairs bedroom on the second level was perfect for the girls. Last year, she and Luke had knocked out a wall of an adjacent room to make a bedroom bigger. For the baby they'd been expecting, they'd painted it a soft, eggshell white, and she'd chosen a white fabric with a design of peach teddy bears for curtains and the padded window seat. But unlike newborns, two-year-olds climbed on everything. "The window seat will have to go," she said, sharing her thought. She glanced toward the window to check on the twins.

Warm from his repeated treks to the truck, Luke dropped onto the closest kitchen chair. "I'll have to contact someone to take it out and finish the wall."

As he relaxed, Val grew more anxious. They had to talk, really talk. There was no time left. "Luke, about the promise we made to Joe and Carrie—" She bit her bottom lip, caught the nervous gesture and stopped. Be honest. It was the only way to deal with the problem. "I'd forgotten about the trip to Joe and Carrie's lawyer—about signing the paper giving us guardianship."

So had he, for a while. They were in an odd situation. The agreed-on divorce threatened a promise to friends, one that had been made when their marriage had been perfect. With a look up, he caught the hint of uncertainty in Val's eyes. Not knowing what she was trying to say, he felt impatience poking at him. "You don't want the responsibility?"

Val needed to backtrack only a few months to realize why he'd asked the question. No children, she'd told him on their wedding anniversary in July when he'd suggested another baby. "We told them that we'd take care of their children if anything happened to them," she said instead of answering him. She believed promises should be kept. At one time, Luke had even teased her about being a little obsessed with the subject. Perhaps she was, just to prove she wasn't like her mother who had made hundreds of promises and kept none.

"Okay." He took a long swig of his ice tea. "So what's your plan now?"

Tenseness coiled around her. "I don't really know," Val said truthfully, standing by the back door and watching the girls. During the past week she'd been thinking mostly about the twins' immediate welfare. "I plan to stay home—for a while. Right now, they need nurturing and stability. If you can get another receptionist, I could handle the accounting at home. Do you think Neil or Lionel would mind?"

It was typical of her to be thinking about others, not herself or how what she was suggesting might personally affect her. "They'll mind that you're not there to deal with their patients." The dentist and podiatrist he shared an office building with thought the world of her. "But they'll understand." Over the rim of his glass, he studied her, wondering if she remembered they had only temporary guardianship. Lovely with the hint of sunlight shining on her, bathing her face with a golden glow, she looked younger than thirty-two at the moment. "You haven't forgotten that there's going to be a home study and a court hearing, have you?"

Val knew all that. "I remember." What she didn't know was how he felt about being a surrogate daddy. Why had everything seemed so simple while they'd been at Joe and Carrie's home packing the twins' belongings?

Luke clicked the ice cubes in his glass. Instinct told him she was fretting. He couldn't alleviate her worry. They were facing a major snag to keep a well-intended promise to friends. "And there's that stipulation in their will to think about. Did you forget it?"

Hardly. Between almost every other thought since she'd cuddled the twins on the night that their parents had died, Val had been thinking about it.

"Our marriage has to be solid for us to get permanent guardianship of the girls." He looked at the dark tea in his glass. "It isn't."

Her hands damp from nerves, Val rubbed one down a denim-clad hip and prodded herself to breach the big problem. "We could pretend."

"What?" Slowly he raised his head. Of all the things he'd imagined she'd say, that wasn't expected.

"Why couldn't we pretend?" Her eyes returned to meet his with a steadiness she didn't feel. "We have to think about the twins." Val drew a hard breath and nervously brushed back strands of her bangs. "I want—I want you to sleep here again, Luke. If you keep sleeping at your office or the hospital, people might notice. We have to consider appearances now.''

He suddenly found himself with forearms on the table, leaning closer. ''What exactly are you suggesting?''

Val felt encouraged. He hadn't given her a flat-out no. He was thinking about the idea. ''We have to look happily married. We have to present the right image of the most perfect couple.'' She sank onto a chair near him. ''For the girls.'' She watched his eyes relax from their narrow stare. ''I don't want them to end up in the system. If we fail, the Department of Health and Social Services will take them from us.'' Even the thought of that happening lumped her throat.

He couldn't ever remember feeling so mentally lost before. ''Do you want to forget the divorce?''

''At least for now,'' she answered, her heart still pounding with fear that he'd say no. In a slow movement, he rubbed a knuckle across his jaw. The contemplating gesture bombarded her with memories and gave her a second of hope. She thought quickly of a way to soften the situation so he wouldn't feel trapped. ''It might be only for three months—six at the most— until the court decides its final recommendations.''

And then what? he nearly asked. Was he supposed to walk away? He cared about the twins, too.

''The girls need us,'' she said softly. ''I know we made a decision but . . .''

Lost in the dark eyes alive with emotion, Luke wasn't unaware of a softening inside him. He resisted it and pushed to a stand. He needed to get away, to think clearly, to make sense of what was happening.

Rather than shower at home, he'd take one at the hospital. "There's a patient I have to check on. And I have ER duty tonight."

His shadowed eyes had revealed nothing to her. Anxious because he hadn't agreed, Val stood. She had no idea what he was thinking. "Is your answer yes or no?"

A palm on the screen door, he paused in pushing it and looked back at her. Logic warred with feelings for her as he saw the appeal in her eyes. How could he refuse? "Yes, I'll do what you asked."

Val waited until the door closed behind him to release the breath she'd been holding. She watched him kiss the girls goodbye. *Let's back up. Start over again.* She couldn't say any of that to him. Too much had happened since February for them to begin again.

Being alone with two-year-old twins should have been a cinch. Val learned differently within minutes.

First Traci yelled, "Pee, pee."

Then Brooke screamed an echo.

Only Brooke made it in time to the potty chair. While changing Traci's soggy diaper, Val saw Brooke limping away with one shoe on and one off.

Val found the missing blue sneaker buried under a doll and the dishtowel Brooke had used as a blanket. By the time she slipped Brooke's sneaker on, Traci had shed both of her shoes and her socks.

Val gave up. On a warm September day, what was the harm in Traci being barefoot in the house?

By six o'clock, she chose a simple dinner of fast-food hamburgers. The girls were thrilled. Val felt guilty. Carrie would have done better for her daughters. But Carrie had eased into the job. For Val, motherhood had been thrust on her. She wasn't complaining. God, no. For most of her life, being a mother had been at the top of her wish list. She simply longed for a little more preparation time.

In a week she'd be supermom, she assured herself. By nature, she was organized. Being an accountant had reinforced those traits. Though everything was a little chaotic and cluttered right now, she was confident that the house would be shipshape by tomorrow and she'd have a schedule in place.

After dinner, Val dug the twins' favorite books out of a box. She ignored the three boxes she'd dumped to find those books. With a promise of bedtime stories, she maneuvered the girls into the bathtub.

Traci howled for her rubber duck.

"Tomorrow," Val promised, soaping Traci through squinting eyes as Brooke splashed water at her. With her blouse soaked and water dripping from her face, she gathered the twins in her arms. They smelled sweet and kissable. Blue eyes drooped slightly, encouraging Val with a thought that sleep might come quickly for them.

After tucking them into bed, she read their books. They were both sleeping before she finished the first story.

Collapsing on a chair in the living room, she swept a glance around at the boxes, at the dumped books, at the toys strewn everywhere. Tomorrow she would clean up the mess.

Exhausted, it took effort to haul herself up the stairs. She was only a step from the doorway when the phone rang. With a dash to the bed, she belly flopped across it and snatched up the receiver before the ringing woke the girls. "Hello?"

"It's me. How's it going?" Luke asked in a soft, considerate tone that used to melt her heart. "Is everything all right?"

No way would she let him know how pooped she was. "Just super."

"Can you manage alone?"

"Of course," she answered because she had little choice. She knew he couldn't be home. She accepted, in fact, admired his conscientiousness about patients. He was a good doctor. She thought he was one of the best in New Hope, in all of Texas.

"Okay. I'll see you in the morning."

Val dropped the receiver into its cradle. Somehow she and Luke would find a way to work things out. They had to—to protect the twins.

Tiredness seeping into her, she yawned and glanced at the bedside clock. Eight-thirty. It was too early for bed, but she needed to rest, to close her eyes.

She slept. How long, she wasn't sure, but a moaning cry jarred her awake. It took less than a second to orient herself as alarm shocked her system. She bolted from the bed, and in a panic, raced down the hall, not even bothering to grab her robe.

The dim light from the lamp that was shaped like a colorful air balloon reflected on Traci, sitting in her crib, tears streaming down her cheeks.

Val scurried to her. "Honey, what's wrong?"

As she lifted her up, Traci's arms wrapped around her neck and clung. "Hold Traci."

Poor little thing. She was frightened. Perhaps she didn't even know why. Until this moment, the twins had asked for their parents a few times, and because of the brief attention span typical of their age, they'd been easily distracted. Luke had told her not to expect grief. He'd explained that at their age, it was too hard for them to show more than passing feelings that would be too sad.

"I'm here," Val nearly cried as she hugged Traci closer and sat on a rocking chair. She stroked her hair soothingly, felt her little body heave as she caught back sobs.

In the other crib, clutching her teddy bear, Brooke stirred but didn't awaken.

With her fingertips, Val blotted the tears from Traci's cheeks.

"Vali stay?"

"Yes, I'll stay."

She snuggled closer, burying her face in Val's neck. "Luke, too?" she asked, then yawned.

Val peered down at her. Her lashes flickered on her cheeks before her eyes closed. For a long moment Val watched the rise and fall of Traci's small chest. How unfair life was. "We're going to be real close and take care of both of you," she whispered.

Gently, Val rocked Traci in the chair that she and Luke had bought in February to soothe their own child. The baby she'd held only once, not in this room with its wallpaper of dancing teddy bears. But in a stark, white hospital room before she'd died.

Chapter Two

Duel wails jolted Val from sleep. Blinking, she peeked at the digital alarm clock on the bedside table, then swung her legs over the side of the bed. How could they be awake at six in the morning? They'd scampered and scurried all day yesterday. They should have been exhausted. She was.

While hurrying toward the bedroom where the twins had slept last night, she shrugged into her robe. Whimpering, Brooke, the quieter of the two, cuddled her teddy bear and sat with her legs dangling between the crib railings. Traci, howling with her eyes closed, had swung a leg over the top railing of the crib.

"Good morning," Val called to them from the doorway. "Are you hungry?"

Traci's eyes popped open, and she squealed with glee.

Brooke's head shot up. So did her arms. "Vali, Vali."

Turning down Main Street, Luke ran a hand across tired eyes after a night of emergency room duty at New Hope General.

At six in the morning, the town was stumbling awake. As usual, Sue Ellen shuffled along the sidewalk to the door of the diner. She yawned, an indication she'd had a late night somewhere. Three times divorced, the good-natured diner owner had taken the time to manipulate her ashy-blond hair into its skyhigh style and had raccooned her eyes. No doubt she would come into his office in a few weeks complaining in her airy manner that she was always tired. Luke often gave her the same response. Get more sleep. And she always laughed as if he had a screw loose for suggesting she miss her nightlife.

Driving past New Hope Park, he negotiated onto the first street on the left. As usual, his mother's kitchen light was on. A before-dawn riser, she'd supply what he needed most at the moment—a good cup of coffee.

She expected him. Though she lived only blocks from his house, she'd become so involved in volunteer work and her part-time job at the New Hope Hotel that seeing her had become a hit-and-miss situation. So Luke visited her at daybreak on the mornings after ER duty.

"I got a letter from Joshua," she said, gesturing with her head toward the envelope on the kitchen counter.

Luke doubted he could focus his eyes to decipher his kid brother's scrawl. "His first letter of the new semester?"

With a hand, Irene smoothed down her sandy blond hair. Plump, with delicate-looking features, she appeared a decade younger than her fifty-eight. "Yes, but he did call me last week."

Luke dropped into a chair at the kitchen table. "A request for money?"

His mother returned his smile. "A little. He likes his new roommate. And he met a girl."

"Already?" Luke shook his head. His twenty-year-old brother made him feel ancient, but sixteen years separated them. Luke had changed his diapers, taught him how to ride a bike and throw a ball, delivered the mandatory birds and bees talk and nudged him toward college. "He's a fast worker."

Her eyes sparkling, Irene teased, "If I remember correctly, you were the same way when in college. Lots of girls. I thought you'd never marry."

"I had too much schooling to deal with to get serious about anyone." Responsibility was something he'd never shied from. When his father had died, he'd been seventeen. He'd assumed the position as head of the household, sheltering his grief-stricken mother from menial tasks and the hoards of bills left after his father's illness. He'd become the substitute father for his kid brother.

Later he'd worked his tail off to put himself through medical school. He understood about hard work and obligations and fighting for what he wanted.

His mother poured another cup of coffee and settled on a chair across the table from him. "Everyone in town believed you'd stay a bachelor, and then Valerie came to town to see her grandfather. I can't tell you how many times I've thanked Edwin for having such a lovely granddaughter," she said with genuine affection.

Luke decided silence might be best since his mother was in such a reminiscing mood.

"Anyone could see how perfect you two were for each other. Agnes always says that my son and his wife are New Hope's model couple."

Luke narrowed an eye. "Agnes, along with her bosom buddies Minny and Ethel, have something to say about everyone."

"Now be kind," his mother admonished lightly. "They're very sweet."

"Busybodies."

"Yes, that, too." Her smile weakened. "About the twins. Everyone is still in shock." She picked up a spoon, then set it down. "I can't believe that Joe and Carrie are gone. It was so tragic, so quick. During the funeral, I felt as if there had to be a mistake. Those poor little girls orphaned like that."

Luke nodded, still dealing with his own grief for good friends.

"It's good that Joe and Carrie considered all possibilities and had you and Valerie legally declared guardians if something happened to them." Slowly she stirred sugar into her coffee now. "I'd hate to imagine them living with Joe's cousin. Charlene Evans is nothing but a—"

"Easy, Mom," he cut in before she got too keyed up.

"Well, she is." Primly she lifted her chin a touch. "She's too self-centered to care about anyone except herself, so it's good she's not involved." She pursed her lips in the manner of someone struggling for silence.

Luke didn't doubt she was mentally delivering a one-on-one to Charlene.

Taking a deep breath, she deliberately softened her voice to indicate her anger had ebbed. "What will you and Valerie do now?"

Luke raked his fingertips across the stubble on his jaw. He wanted to ease the conversation in another direction. Though it hadn't been easy, somehow he and Val had managed to keep their troubled marriage a private matter from everyone except Val's grandfather and Jenny Stevens. McCord, soon, he reminded himself. She'd be Jenny McCord next year. "Mom, it's too early in the morning for questions."

Both impatience and worry clouded her eyes. "Valerie isn't still enthusiastic about moving to Dallas, is she?"

He raised his head slowly. Dumbfounded that she even knew about Val's plans, he tried to veil his surprise.

"I'd hoped she'd changed her mind since she'd mentioned that before what happened—before you got the twins," she said to clarify what she meant. "When Valerie mentioned she wanted to move, she also said she didn't think you'd want to go."

Luke picked up quickly on what had happened. His wife had been preparing his mother for what seemed inevitable. Because of irrevocable differences, her son and his wife were divorcing. Obviously the conversation hadn't reached that stage and his mother only believed they had a slight problem in their perfect marriage.

"I assured her you two would come to some agreement. Dallas is only thirty miles away." She bounded to a stand to refill his coffee cup, and rambled on. "Why couldn't you two live in Dallas, and you commute to New Hope? I mean, I understand your practice is here but—"

"She wants to go to Houston, not Dallas." When Val had made the announcement, he'd been stunned. She'd known he wouldn't budge from New Hope. He'd always said that he never planned to live anywhere else. From the first day they'd met over four years ago, he'd told her that after medical school he'd chosen to pass on big money positions and return to the town where he'd been born and raised.

"You're moving and I'm not," he'd said to her. "What now?"

Only one answer had made sense—divorce.

Then the phone had rung, shattering the silence between them. That phone call had changed everything. Shock had slammed at them when they'd learned Carrie and Joe had died. Suddenly they'd been of one mind for the first time in too long as they'd asked the same question. "Where are the twins?"

"You have the twins to consider now," his mother said, cutting into his thoughts.

Luke raised his eyes to her as he took several sips of the steaming brew she'd set in front of him.

She pulled her chenille robe tighter before sitting again. As a kid, he'd sat like this with her early in the morning before he would head out to deliver newspapers. "You and Val will apply for permanent guardianship, and eventually adopt them, won't you?"

Luke stalled, not certain what was in the future. Quickly he offered an explanation to prevent a rash of questions. "There are a lot of things to think about." Before she delved deeper, he drained the coffee in his cup, then pecked her cheek with a kiss. "Talk to you soon."

He hadn't been evasive with her. He honestly didn't know what was going to happen.

Within minutes he pulled into the driveway at home. Having caught only snatches of sleep at the hospital, he wondered if he could grab a few hours in bed before the twins awakened. He opened the back door that led into the kitchen and walked into chaos.

Val stood with her back to him, straddling Traci's high chair. "You have to sit or I can't feed you."

Stiffening, the little one yelled, waving her arms, and balked at sitting.

In her high chair, Brooke banged on the tray, her eyes darting to him. "Lu-cas. Me up."

Startled, Val swung around. She hadn't expected him home yet. In need of a shave, with his hair tousled from the wind, he carried the look of morning.

While she'd been daydreaming, he'd moved closer. "You stay down. And you sit down," he said firmly to Traci, plunking her into the high chair. Quickly, he fastened the strap. "I didn't expect them up yet," he admitted to Val.

Val stifled amusement. He'd be in for a rude awakening tomorrow then, when he learned dawn was their wake-up time. "They get up very early."

What Luke thought was humor in her voice made him turn his head. She seemed different to him. Brighter in spirit, her smiles coming easily, like they used to. Or was she just making the best of this situation?

"Me up," Brooke insisted again.

"Traci up," her sister echoed.

Over her shoulder, Val sent him a now-you're-in-for-it look.

"Why don't I read a book while we wait for breakfast," he suggested.

Val gladly relinquished the task of quieting them and busied herself getting their breakfast.

"Hat. Cat in hat," Brooke yelled.

Traci shook her head adamantly. "Big Bird book."

"The hat book now and—" He paused as Traci's face squinched up in preparation to wail. "And the Big Bird book when you're done eating."

Traci's features relaxed. She blew out a breath, thrusting out her lower lip. Since silence reigned, he viewed the pout as acceptance and rummaged in a box in the kitchen corner for the books. "You didn't get them settled in yet?"

"It's taking more time than I expected." Val didn't mention that bedlam had prevailed last night before bedtime while she'd searched in cartons for Brooke's teddy bear and Traci's doll.

Luke frowned into the carton of books. He should have been home with her. Was she thinking he was never near when she needed him?

"Lu-cas read." Brooke patted his shoulder to grab his attention.

Guilt closing in on him, he looked down to concentrate on the pages of the book, but that wasn't easy. Nothing made sense suddenly. They were ready to divorce, yet he was as aware of his wife now as he'd been when they were first married. Slanting a look in her direction, he watched her reach for the cereal. The silky material of her short robe clung to her hips. Then the hem raised, exposing a shapely thigh. A shimmer of heat slowly inching down him, Luke leaned back in his chair. Spending time with her—pretending—was going to be harder than he'd expected.

While he rattled the last of the tongue-twister rhymes, Val set a bowl of cereal and a spoon in front of each twin. With her closeness, he nearly fingered her hair. Whether it was crazy or not, he found himself thinking about touching her.

Relaxed, Val grabbed her first sip of coffee since awakening and lounged against the counter. She could handle moments like this with Luke, she told herself. For the twins' sake, they would pretend.... A quick, familiar grin curved his lips, nearly undoing her. That he was looking at the twins didn't seem to matter. Something fluttered inside her.

"If you can deal with this alone for a little while, I thought I'd go to the hardware store," he said, dropping the books back into the carton.

It took her a moment to concentrate on what he was saying. Was he really offering to spend time doing odd jobs? "Aren't you going into the office later this morning?"

"No. Besides dead bolts on the doors, what do you want done?" Out of natural reflex, he stared expectantly at her. A trait learned as a husband. There were times when her decisions outranked his, like now.

Val had planned to call Pete Armstrong who, for a minimal fee, would have done the safety proofing of the house. With Luke's offer, she didn't have the heart to suggest that to him now. But Mr. Handyman, he wasn't. "I thought locks for the cabinets, including special ones for the medicine cabinets, and those shields for the sockets."

"Do you want a gate of some sort for the bedroom to keep them from wandering all over the place?" His voice trailed off and his gaze shifted toward Traci.

Bent to the side, she was happily watching cereal plop from her spoon onto the floor.

"Traci, no." Val dashed for the paper towel roll, then dropped to her knees to mop up the mess.

"Don't you think you should—?" Luke shut up as she snapped a fiery look at him. After *he* moved the cereal out of Traci's reach and took the spoon from her, he snatched a wad of the toweling to join Val on the floor. "I'll take those," he said about the soggy paper towels in her hand.

"Thanks." She wasn't angry about the mess. Her problem was him. She supposed she'd simply have to get used to having him around so much. Feeling less irritable, she searched for conversation. "Will you have time to childproof everything today?"

"I'll have time." Last night he'd thought long and hard about a lot of things, including his role in the failure of their marriage. He'd let her down too much already.

"If you can't do it all today, tomorrow—" As he reached for the wet paper towels in her hand, his fingers brushed hers. Her breath hitched, pleasure bubbling up within her so quickly she had no time to block it.

"I'll have time today," Luke insisted, answering with a casualness that took effort.

"Good." Val masked emotion with a reminder. It was normal to still feel twinges of desire. Whatever old emotions were stirring would level off.

On his way to the door, Luke tossed the soaked paper into the wastebasket. "I shouldn't take too long at the hardware store." Not expecting a response from her, he fished the car keys from the pocket of his Levi's. The announcement he'd put off since arriving home was long overdue. Stopping at the door, he faced her. "I'm taking a few days off."

"What?" She wasn't sure that was a good idea. Pretending was one thing. Being together too much might cause some difficult moments.

"I traded duty in the emergency room at the hospital. And I talked to Fred Henderson about seeing patients I had appointments with at the office this week."

Val sensed by the hint of amusement in his eyes that she looked the way she felt—stunned. "Why are you doing this?"

Why was he? To help? To ease some old feelings he'd never totally gotten rid of? He answered as honestly as he could. "This is as new to you as it is to me. And we need to get them settled in."

She stood, staring after him, and feeling confused. An eternity had passed since they'd worked hard together toward a goal.

* * *

Throughout the morning, though the twins behaved, they were a handful to keep an eye on. Carrying a clean set of sheets, Val entered the master bedroom. Quickly she stripped the bed and, gathering the sheets, dumped them into the clothes hamper. Merrily, Traci was jumping on the mattress. Spotting Val, she romped through the blanket and bedspread that were heaped at a corner as if they were her private tunnel.

Amused, Val lifted her off and set her on the floor. Her back to the door, she heard the pitter-patter of feet and swung around to see Brooke barreling onto the bed and rolling herself in the blanket. Val grabbed her. With Brooke in her arms, she turned back to Traci. Across the hall now, in their room, she was tearing her way through the small stuffed animals in a carton and flinging them into the hallway.

With a small shake of her head, Val snatched Traci in her other arm. Sitting both girls against the wall, she pointed her finger at them. "Don't move until I tell you."

Identical faces with sparkling eyes appealed to her. Marshmallow, Val mused. Scooping up both of them, she fell back on the bed and was rewarded with the sound of their laughter as they bounced on the mattress.

By 11:30 she'd finished making the beds and vacuuming. Phone calls from friends slowed Val's progress at making lunch. She thanked them all for their offers to help her and gave assurances she had everything under control. Of course, she didn't.

"Lu-cas, Lu-cas," Brooke yelled, barreling through the kitchen when she heard the sound of a car door slamming. The moment he stepped in, she lunged at him and clung to his denim-clad leg.

A bag cradled in one arm, he ran his other hand over the crown of silky blond hair. "What are you and Traci doing?"

"Nutin'." She flashed a saintly smile that only a two year old could get away with.

"Nutin', huh?" He responded to her need for affection and dropped to her level to pull her into his arms. "You've been good?"

Her head bobbed dramatically. As she smacked a kiss on his cheek, he set the bag on the floor. Like a welcoming signal, Traci leapt at him. Luke caught her in his other arm and cuddled her, too.

Val felt her heart squeeze and turned away from the sight of the three of them hugging. Somewhere deep inside him still existed all the tenderness and warmth that had seemed to disappear during the past months. Yet she'd lost touch with that man, with what he felt, what he was worried or pleased about. She hadn't known that man since the day their daughter had died, since the day he'd drawn inside himself, shutting her out.

She looked up from the vegetables she was chopping to stir-fry for lunch and saw two blond toddlers trailing him out of the room.

Half an hour later, Val finished carting the rest of the stuffed animals to a cabinet in the twins' bedroom and glanced at the clock. Engrossed in what she'd been doing, she'd nearly forgotten lunch.

With the rice steaming, she searched the first floor, then climbed the stairs. Hearing voices in one of the bathrooms, she slowed her stride.

"Whatsat?" Brooke asked, peering over Luke's arm.

Luke clamped a hand over the screwdriver before Brooke's fingers closed over it. "A screwdriver."

"Scewdiver," Traci said in his ear, draping herself over his back and strangleholding him with her arms. "Traci do it."

"No, I'll do it," Luke informed her.

While the girls badgered him with questions, he never missed a beat. He kept working, his voice calm as he answered each one.

Peering down at his hands, Traci pressed her cheek against his. "Why?"

"Because it should be locked."

"Why?" Brooke asked now, bending forward over his arm again to get a better view of what he was doing.

Val decided to rescue him. "Is anyone hungry?"

"Hungry," the girls responded in unison.

Holding out a hand toward the twins, Val enticed them with a job. "We have to set the table." As they charged for her legs, she braced herself for the jolt. "Will you be done here in a few minutes?" she asked Luke.

"Go ahead and start without me."

Despite his intent to keep working and avoid the cozy lunch, he joined them a few minutes later. Spills and childish chatter kept the moments free of these silences between Val and him that he wanted to avoid.

After a lively half-hour of lunchtime chatter, he resumed the job of covering wall sockets in his den. From the vicinity of a bathroom upstairs, wails resounded through the rooms. What now? he wondered. Choosing a nail to hook up the venetian blind cord, he grabbed a hammer.

As he whacked at the nail, he heard footsteps and looked away. Bent over, Val was digging into a toy box. For no more than a second, his attention strayed to her, but that was all the time needed. A sharp pain burst through the tip of his finger. "Dammit!" Wincing, he looked down at the fingernail he'd struck.

"Uh-oh," two voices rang out from behind him. Frowns in place, the girls cornered him. Brooke wagged a finger while her mirror image shook her head disapprovingly. "Bad."

"Yes, very bad," he muttered. Still the recipient of two disapproving looks, he delivered a final whack at the intended object.

Staring up at him, Brooke tipped her head. "Ow-ee?"

"No. No, ow-ee. Why don't you two go play?"

Brooke shook her head. "No ow-ee," she told her sister before whipping around and racing ahead of Traci toward the door. "Want ball."

"No!" Traci yelled, dashing after her.

Staring at him from her bent-over position, Val thought he'd shown amazing self-control with the girls so near. "Are you all right?"

Hardly. How could he be? Her scooped-neck T-shirt still bellowed to offer him a seductive view of the lace on her bra and the swell of breasts above it. "Fine," he grumbled, as distracted as before. Idly his gaze traveled over her. "Did you have another crisis in the bathroom?"

"Yes." A little breathless, she straightened and told herself that she was imagining the provocative once-over. "It was about the toilet," she answered, more steady when he looked away to raise the cord on the blinds to a hook that little hands couldn't reach.

Leaning back, Luke smiled wryly, baffled because he would swear he'd heard screams, signaling tears. "What about it?"

"They both wanted the job of flushing it." Determined to stop acting like a fool, she eyed a spot for the toy box then hustled across the room for a tape measure.

If he didn't know better, Luke would have said she was moving with nervous energy. But why would she be nervous? With a shake of his head, he packed up the toolbox. He was proving to be his own worst enemy.

"It's too quiet, isn't it?" she asked, making him aware that she'd paused in stretching out the tape measure.

"I'll check," he volunteered. It might be smart not to be alone with her too much. Whatever yearnings he felt weren't part of the agreement.

From the bottom of the stairs, he looked up and saw Traci in the hallway running toward the steps. Luke waited at the bottom one. Head down, she clung to the railing and cautiously descended the six steps. As her small foot met the last step, she bumped into him. Her head jerked up. Blue eyes shot him a look of innocence that he didn't believe. "What have you been doing?" he asked, lifting her into his arms.

Because she answered with a giggle, Luke climbed the steps. "Where's your partner in mischief?" She didn't need to tell him. He found Brooke on the floor of the master bedroom beside the telephone.

Seeing him, she dropped the receiver and scooted past him out the door.

"Down. Down," Traci insisted, wiggling in his arms.

He thought twice about it. One on the loose could get in enough trouble. "Go watch television," he instructed before lowering her to the floor. As she scurried away, he replaced the telephone receiver, then did a damage survey of the room. Seeing nothing dumped or broken, he strolled out.

"Are they up here?" Val called to him, standing at the top of the stairs.

He'd thought they'd both gone downstairs. "No, I—"

She took off before he could finish and sailed into one bathroom. "They have to be downstairs," she yelled at him.

He followed, reaching the bottom step to see her dashing toward the kitchen. Luke chose a different path of searching, and relied on sound. Soft giggles drifting to him, when Val reappeared, he pointed toward his den. "They're in there," he said in a low voice.

Contently the twins sat on the floor near his desk, emptying drawers and tossing around papers.

At being caught in the act, Brooke simply grinned, but Traci scrambled to a stand and raced to Val to tug on her hand. "Pee, pee."

Luke had his doubts. "It's a diversion."

"Could be," Val agreed, not missing both laughter and skepticism in his voice. "But I can't take a chance that it is."

Alone with Brooke, Luke set her in front of her toy computer and started picking up the papers. He looked away from her for no more than a minute. When he looked back, she was gone.

He crossed the room in a few long strides and visually scanned the dining and living rooms. With a turn, he spotted her climbing from the kitchen stool onto the counter. Taking no chances, he hit the floor on a skid and snagged her before she lost her balance.

Leaning back against the counter, he recalled that he'd been feeling guilty about missing his morning run lately. With them around, he didn't need an exercise program. "Go by your sister," he said, seeing Val setting Traci down in front of the television set.

After putting the stool into the utility closet and out of the temptation of little hands, he reclaimed his toolbox from the other room.

By one-thirty, he'd almost finished with the locks on kitchen cabinets.

"I'll never get organized," Val muttered, entering the kitchen from the garage.

In a far corner of the room, Traci crawled through one of the large, empty boxes. "Be a doggie, Brooke."

"Moo-moo."

Luke's chuckle lifted Val's head from a carton of dollhouse furniture. She assumed it was because she hadn't heard the sound in so long that it warmed her instantly. She started to smile but didn't. He wasn't looking at the girls now. He was staring at her in a way too familiar for her to pretend it was a casual glance.

Her heart beating faster, she raked her fingers through her short strands. In a few hours she'd learned one thing for certain. The constant nearness after not being around each other for so long was going to cause a few problems. "If you're going to be in here for a while longer, I'm going to put some of the clothes in dressers."

"I'll keep an eye on them." As she swept by, like a wave of freshness, her scent floated over him. Luke inhaled deeply, absorbing it. If she wanted to play fair, she wouldn't wear that damn perfume.

In between fastening safety locks on the sliding-glass door, he checked on the girls. Still trailing each other through the box, they tooted and shrieked what sounded to him like choo-choo. Assured they were occupied, he returned to the job he'd started. Only a few moments passed.

"Luke!" Rather than alarm, he heard urgency in his wife's voice.

What could be wrong now? He dropped the screwdriver into the toolbox and in three strides reached the stairs. "What's wrong?"

She flew down the steps, past him and dashed to the kitchen. "The toilet overflowed."

Luke followed to find her rummaging in the utility closet. "What did you do?"

She stepped out of the closet, holding a mop and a bucket filled with rags. Strands of hair around her face glistened with moisture. Her soaked T-shirt clung like a second skin. "I found the water shutoff valve," she said before sprinting past him.

That wasn't what he'd meant, but he was glad she had. He didn't have any idea where the damn thing was located. Taking two steps at a time, he climbed the steps to catch up with her. "Dropped too much paper into it again, did you?"

Not thrilled at his assumption that she was the guilty party, Val tipped up her chin and swung a slow look back at him. "Excuse me," she said tightly.

At the landing, he fell into step beside her. "I thought we'd worked this out. When you do your ritual..."

She fired a withering look up at him. "My ritual?"

"When you cream your face, dump the tissue in the waste—"

"It's two in the afternoon," she cut in. "Why would I be cleaning my face?"

That shut him up.

So did the puddle on the bathroom floor.

Standing beside her outside the bathroom door, he said the obvious. "It's wet in there."

Val had the good sense not to say what she was thinking. "Here's the plunger." She thrust it at him, then stripped off her sneakers and socks to mop the floor.

"Damn." Yanking off his socks, he kept staring at the floor as if he'd never seen water before. "How could one of them have gotten up here without being noticed? I thought they were playing with the box the whole time."

Head bent, Val slopped the mop around on the floor to dry up the excess water. "They're wily."

Barefoot, he squeezed by her. "They're only two."

"It's a trait learned at an early age," she said, wringing the mop water into a bucket.

While he shoved his arm into the toilet water, he grumbled, "These hands aren't meant for this."

Val bit back a laugh. "What was thrown in there?" she asked in her best serious tone under the circumstances.

Scowling, Luke withdrew his arm and held up a bright orange plastic dinosaur.

He looked so disdainful at the toy that Val barely stifled her grin. "Did you get toilet seat clamps when you were at the hardware store?"

"They're in the bag."

She thought it wise to leave before she began to laugh. "I'll get them." She hurried down the steps but paused long enough to see the twins still tunneling through the box. She returned to him and the sound of the toilet flushing. "All fixed?"

His lips curved in a slow-spreading smug smile.

Machismo was alive and well, Val mused. He'd made one simple household repair and acted as if he belonged on the television sitcom "Home Improvement." "I'll mop first, then you can put on these clamps. But I have to get downstairs. They can't be alone too long."

"An understatement." Unexpected humor colored his tone. "We're learning that, aren't we?" His voice trailed off.

Val knew why. Quietness meant trouble. She whipped around. One step into the hallway, she stopped.

Without her saying a word, Luke guessed some disaster had struck. "What now?" he asked, joining her in the hallway.

Zigzagging in and out of rooms, Traci madly dashed with toilet paper trailing her.

"Where do you think Brooke is?" Val asked with a glance toward the stairs.

Luke charged for their bedroom. Rarely were the twins far apart.

Enjoying herself, Brooke sat on the floor in the master bedroom, busily dumping a wastebasket.

"Which one's mess do you want to clean up?" Val asked from behind him in the doorway.

"Call it," Luke said on a laugh.

"I'll take the toilet paper queen."

Chapter Three

"Who bombed this place?"

Carrying the mop and bucket to the kitchen, Luke swiveled a look at the gray-haired man standing at the front door. Amusement sparkled in Edwin's brown eyes while he scanned the messy living room.

From the stairs, Val made an excuse about the disarray. "Gramps, we don't have them settled in yet."

Slowly he hunkered down to where the twins were playing with blocks. "What could take so long? Two tykes like this can't bring much with them."

Luke chuckled, drawing a frown from Val.

"Keep your eyes on them for a minute," she requested, wanting to change her damp T-shirt.

"Do you want coffee or an ice tea?" Luke asked her grandfather.

Trailing him into the kitchen, Edwin played out a moment of hesitation before answering. "You choose. And I'll choose the topic of conversation."

Crusty, Edwin never failed to amuse Luke. "I bet you will," he said, giving Edwin a tolerant smile as he closed the door of the utility closet.

Edwin's bushy gray brows rose above the top of his wire-rimmed glasses. "While we're alone, I want to discuss my granddaughter." As if pained, he pushed his glasses forward and massaged the bridge of his nose. "This divorce is a dumb decision. You never said. Is it your idea or hers?" he asked, shoving his glasses back.

"I don't remember." Luke avoided placing blame. Too much fell on him.

"How can you not remember something that important? Never mind, never mind. I'll tell you what you have to do." Suddenly on a roll, he added, "You need to win your wife back. And you'd better do something before some other guy muscles in." As the girls tramped in, Edwin retrieved a soft peppermint candy for each girl from his shirt pocket.

Thank-you's came in unison.

"You have an advantage, Luke," Edwin mumbled while shoving a peppermint into his mouth. Sucking on the candy, he offered a closed-lip grin at Luke and started stacking the blocks that the girls had brought in with them. Blond heads tipping, the twins watched intently.

"What's that?" Luke asked.

"Love."

Love doesn't seem to be enough, Luke wanted to tell him.

"Just so you don't think I'm picking on you, let me tell you that I told her the same thing."

Luke couldn't stop himself from asking. "What did she say?"

Edwin grimaced. "Nothing. That's what she said. Nothing."

Preparing himself for an onslaught of advice, Luke sat back in his chair and decided to lighten his own mood by enjoying Edwin's spiel.

"Sometimes people—" Edwin silenced in midsentence as the girls toppled the tower of blocks he'd just built. He started again. "Sometimes people have no sense," he muttered. "They make problems for themselves." He restacked the blocks, then looked up, frowning. "Don't you have any understanding of my problems?"

Warily, Luke narrowed his eyes. "I wasn't aware that you had problems."

"Of course, you are. Few of my friends can even stand the men that their daughters or granddaughters married. I was one of the lucky ones."

Luke chuckled. "You do have a smooth tongue, old man."

"I'm not paying any attention to your snide remarks. Face it," he insisted, "You were damn lucky, too. You got my granddaughter."

Luke had always thought he was. Val had been all he'd ever wanted. "Everything is different," he answered. "And you know why. You know what went wrong."

"But in time—"

"Nothing is that simple," Luke reminded him.

"All I'm asking," Edwin appealed, "is to consider what I suggested."

Puzzled, Luke looked up. "And what is that?"

"Romance." Edwin regarded him with a thoughtful expression. "Romance her."

Luke laughed. Edwin never failed to surprise him.

"Win your wife back," Edwin said slowly as if Luke were mentally slow. "It's—" His attention zeroed in on the stairs and Val's descent. "It's a great idea."

Catching the end of the conversation, Val paused before entering the kitchen. "What's a great idea?" That her grandfather avoided looking at her assured her he was definitely up to something.

"That I come back tomorrow and help out."

"Why not now?" she questioned while handing Brooke the Raggedy Ann doll from the counter that she was stretching to reach.

"And miss Monday night football?" he asked as if she were crazy.

On a laugh, Val waved her hand. "'Bye, then."

"'Bye, sweetie." He planted a quick kiss on her cheek on his way to the door. "You got company," he called back, leaving the door open.

"Hi." Irene breezed in with a giant-size panda under each arm and a shopping bag dangling from her wrist.

It took little brain power for Val to guess her mother-in-law had come bearing goodies and a determination to spoil the twins.

They rushed to Irene, eyeing the pandas. "One for each of you."

Hugging hers, Traci gazed up at Irene over the panda's shoulder and wrapped her other arm around Irene's leg. "Tank you."

Like a beaming, proud grandparent, Irene ran a hand over Traci's cornsilk hair. "You're welcome."

More restrained, Brooke had yet to accept her panda.

Val knew that Irene would be patient. Carrie had gained celebrity status after she'd had the twins. Everyone who'd known the Dawsons had oohed and aahed about the twins from the day Carrie had brought them home from the hospital. With each passing day, those same people had noticed Brooke tended to approach people more cautiously, to contemplate each new adventure, while Traci, the extrovert, plunged impulsively forward.

"I'll carry it for you for now," Irene suggested, not rushing Brooke to accept her gift.

That earned Irene a slim smile from the little one.

"What are you playing with?" Irene asked.

"Dolls," Traci answered.

"Oh, I love dolls. Do you have others?" With Traci's nod, Irene beamed at her. "Will you show me where they are?"

"Irene." Val hated to ruin Irene's fun, but she recalled how Carrie had always said that a missed naptime meant an evening with Cranky and Crabby. "It's naptime."

"Oh, is it?" Her eyes fixed on the twins, Irene kept smiling. "Well, you and Lucas sit down, have a cup of coffee or a glass of ice tea and relax. Come on, girls." Irene snagged a small hand in each of her own and urged the twins to the stairs. "Show me your room."

Traci raised big blue eyes to Irene. "Polly's there."

Irene had had enough contact with the girls to know that Polly was Traci's baby doll. "I imagine Polly is already napping."

Traci bobbed her head agreeably.

"That's good." At the stairs, Irene glanced askance. "Valerie, you're not sitting. Sit. I'll put them down."

Val really wanted to. In less than twenty-four hours she'd learned one vital lesson to survival. When the twins rested, so should she, but she felt nervous. With the twins upstairs, safely being watched by Irene, it was just Luke and her again. "I think I'll get some of this picked up."

Her voice had sounded breathy to him. Because of him? Luke wondered.

"Gramps left quickly."

"He had his say."

"And what was that?"

Thoughtfully he studied her. "What you'd expect from him. Basically he told me that I was losing the best thing in my life." With the sole of his sneaker, he nudged at the leg of the chair, pushing it out for her. "Why don't you take a minute to rest?"

Val said nothing. What could she say? *I needed you, and you didn't need me.* She walked into the living room, sank onto the chair and avoided Luke's stare as he followed her. It seemed best to her to keep conversation off the subject of them. "We need to get a bigger toy box."

Luke saw what she did. It looked as if they'd been burglarized. Sofa cushions were strewn, along with toys and dolls, across the plush carpeting. "A moving van parked in the backyard might work." Her smile came quickly, unexpectedly. With effort, he looked away and down at his glass. "Want a sip?"

As he held out his glass to her, she leaned forward for it. They could still be friends, she told herself. No anger or fights had split them. They'd simply drifted apart. So even if their marriage was over, why couldn't they remain friends? Lots of mature people managed such a relationship. "Seriously, do you think we'll ever get this place in order?"

An easy task. It was their life they hadn't been able to put back together. "What's order?"

Val raised her eyes to him. How with a few simple words did he manage to zero in on the crux of the problem? What used to be, no longer existed. "How did Carrie do this? I couldn't have dreamed this would be so difficult, could you? Carrie always looked so in control, so calm."

In his opinion, she wasn't giving herself enough credit. For someone who liked everything in its place, she was handling the messiness with motherly panache. "She came upon this responsibility naturally." As she angled forward to return the glass, his gaze wandered to the strain of cotton at her breasts. Little things kept churning him up. He'd been blocking desire for her, but it was in full force again, he realized. "You're getting them with their motors in high gear."

Val brushed back her bangs. "I didn't have a chance to ask earlier. Is your patient okay? The one you checked on last night."

Unlike some of his colleagues' wives, she'd always revealed a kindness, a caring about the patients, a genuine interest in what he was dealing with. "It was touch and go for a while, but I believe he'll be okay. I have an idea about all this," he said, indicating the mess in the living room.

Consciously she concentrated on relaxing muscles in her shoulders. There was no reason to be so tense. They were talking with ease. That was a good start. "What idea?" she asked, leaning back in her chair.

"The second panda found a bed," Irene suddenly announced, appearing in the doorway and looking pleased that she'd made progress with Brooke. "I hope they'll call me Grandma someday. I didn't want to mention that today, but since they never knew grandparents, it shouldn't be confusing to them to give me that name."

Losing a child had a rippling effect, Luke mused. His mother had been nearly as devastated as he and Val had been. "Everything will take time, Mom."

"Yes, of course. Even instant parenthood. You look frazzled, Valerie."

Val laughed, thinking that was a mild description.

"But how lucky for them to have both of you. Everyone always believed you'd make wonderful par—" She cut off the last word, her eyes darting to Luke with a look as if she wanted to cut out her tongue.

Val felt both of them staring at her and delivered her most convincing smile to ease the worry away from Irene's face. Neither Luke nor his mother needed to be concerned. Though it had taken Val months, she'd finally come to terms with the loss of their baby. It was the shock of losing good friends that had made her realize that she couldn't fold up emotionally forever, even if she'd wanted to.

As if anxious to fill the silence, Irene rambled on about the difficulties of moving the twins into their house. "There's always so much to do during a move. You're not still considering one to Houston, are you?" she asked, sounding anxious about the idea.

Val acknowledged she hadn't thought about that decision since the night she'd announced it to Luke. She'd felt then that she needed a fresh start. She needed to go somewhere, anywhere. She'd wanted to get away from New Hope, where her hopes for the future had ended seven months ago. But neither the move nor the divorce mattered at the moment. "After their loss, the girls need security and love. It wouldn't be good to move them right now too far away from what they're familiar with."

"Oh, good." Irene's pleased expression lingered even when her gaze wandered to the unpacked cartons. "Would you like any help?"

"No, we're making headway." Val could have used help, but the pretense between Luke and her would be difficult under Irene's perceptive eye. "But thank you, Irene."

"Oh, any time." She moved to the door. "Just in case, I'll be back tomorrow."

As the door closed behind her, Val eyed empty cartons that needed to go in the garage. She stood but paused. "I'm glad she doesn't know about us," she said before leaving him.

So was he. Luke remembered the worry in his mother's eyes when she'd mentioned their moving. She'd be distraught if she learned of their plans to divorce.

* * *

Within an hour, loud childish singing, an off-key rendition of "Happy Birthday," drifted to Val from the room upstairs, signaling the end of the twins' naptime. She got them up, fed them a light snack, then sought out Luke and suggested a trip to the store for another toy box.

The outing proved more of a feat than Val had anticipated.

By Luke's exasperated expression, he was just as baffled as she was that they were being bamboozled by two-year-olds.

For the third time since they'd entered the store, Luke went after Brooke while Val chased down Traci. Seconds later, he appeared at the end of the aisle that Val had cornered Traci in. "I've got mine," he announced proudly, carrying Brooke on his shoulders.

With Traci perched on her hip, Val heaved a sigh.

"Go home," Traci chanted.

Val kissed her cheek. "A wonderful idea."

"What are we having to eat?" Luke asked almost within seconds after they entered the house.

Val had given dinner no thought. Toys, not food, had been on her mind. After last night's greasy hamburgers, she had planned to serve the twins healthy fare. "Salad and . . ."

"Pizza," the girls yelled.

Mr. Junk Food was no help. "Sounds good to me."

They cheered.

Tying Traci's sneaker, Val suddenly felt like the only adult in the room. "You should lose your medical license. If any of your patients ever knew what a junk food addict you are, they'd never take any of your advice." With some maternal guilt rising, she admitted, "I gave them hamburgers and French fries last night."

"Tomorrow we'll whip up—"

He grew silent. Val knew why. How long had it been since they'd thought in terms of we? "Okay, pizza. But I'm making a salad."

"Yeah, pizza!" The girls dashed into the living room and raced for a small plastic wagon.

"Traci, ride," she yelled.

Val stood still, waiting for the battle to begin. With a peek around the doorjamb, she saw Brooke struggling to pull her sister who was sitting like a queen in her coach. "I don't believe it. They didn't argue," she said while taking plates from a cabinet. "Do you think that once they feel comfortable here, they'll calm down?"

In fascination, Luke watched late-afternoon sunshine dance across Val's hair with her movement between the refrigerator and the counter. "We hope."

"Yes, we hope," she answered. Again the *we*.

If her pulse scrambled a little when he was near, that was natural, Val told herself. She knew so much about him. The way he peppered eggs until a layer of black specks covered them, his weakness for sci-fi movies, his interest in documentaries about animals.

Behind her, he talked on the phone and ordered the pizza. For more times than she could count, she'd listened to his chuckling when he read the comics in the Sunday newspaper, had heard his earthy frustrations when he lost a patient, had melted beneath his caresses and whispered words during lovemaking. All that was him was a part of her. It would be impossible to believe she'd ever forget any of that. But just as she wasn't the same woman he'd married, the man she remembered didn't really exist anymore. Both of those people had gotten lost in a sea of tragedy.

Luke hung the receiver back in its cradle, then pulled out a cutting board and joined her at the counter.

"What was the idea you were going to tell me when Irene came in?" Val asked over the water rushing onto the tomato in her hand.

"The biggest problem we're having is finding a place for all of the twins' toys. Right?"

Val turned off the water and began shredding carrots. "I'd say that was part of the problem."

"Okay, so why don't I give up my den for a playroom?"

She stopped shredding the carrot in her hand. "It's always been a quiet place for you to do work at home. I don't know where you'd go to do that."

"I'll leave my desk there, but we'll set up the rest of the room for the girls. We talked about doing that when you..."

"When I was expecting Kelly." She tried to keep sadness at bay, but a hint of it crept into her voice. "I forgot we were going to do that."

Luke had forgotten nothing of her pregnancy, not the morning sickness or her joy in shopping for baby things, or the difficult labor. Nothing.

Val fought the pressure crowding her throat. She wouldn't dwell on any of that now. "I think it would be a really good idea."

Though her eyes remained solemn, her lips curved in a slim, uncertain smile. There was a strength emerging from her that he hadn't seen in months.

Glancing at the girls seated on the floor and thumbing through picture books, Val visualized the rest of the house returning to normal. This is a big adjustment for all of us, she realized.

"Were you telling my mother the truth about not moving?"

"Yes. Everything has changed. I couldn't go to Houston right now."

"So no move?"

"No move," she answered.

Through dinner, the girls picked at their salads but consumed the pizza with gusto. While tomato sauce only smudged the edges of Brooke's lips, Traci wore it.

Squinching up her nose, Traci peeled an olive off her pizza and handed it to Brooke. "Yucky," she declared.

For no more than a second, Brooke eyed the olive in her hand with pure disgust. "Yucky." Her blond head tipped to the side as she watched the olive's descent to the floor.

Val bent to retrieve the olive while Traci tugged on Luke's sleeve. "Milk, pease." Impatient as usual, she reached for it just as Luke did. The glass tipped, sloshing milk onto the table. "You did it," she scolded him.

Luke couldn't stop a grin.

"Stop that," she said, wagging a finger at him. "Not funny."

In his whole life, he'd never pictured an evening like this, with him being chastised by a two year old.

"Wanna get down," Traci insisted, lifting herself from the high chair seat.

"Awl done," Brooke sang out, raising her arms to Luke.

"You have to wash up before you can play," Val said, picking up Traci.

Already crawling under the table, Brooke noisily dumped blocks.

Val held her arm open to her. "Brooke, come on."

Engrossed in stacking the blocks, Brooke fell back on the floor, indicating she had no intention of doing anything. As if sensing power in unity, Traci copied her sister's actions and howled.

With little choice, Val picked up Brooke. She didn't look back. She heard Traci's wail intensifying and knew Luke had grabbed her.

The bathroom resounded with their blood-curdling cries. But the minute the water rushed from the spigot, both girls quieted and play began. Four little hands floated in the washbasin at the same time. Enthusiastically, the twins lathered soap all over their arms, splashing the sink and the wall.

Her shirt drenched, Val dried their hands and watched them merrily race out of the bathroom as if they'd never caused a ruckus.

"I love a challenge," Luke murmured, yanking off his wet shirt.

Val laughed with him before she stepped into the hallway. "Expect a lot of them," she said, and looked back. Instantly she wished she hadn't. Her gaze shifted to his broad, masculine chest. Smooth and toned and well-muscled. God, he looked wonderful. It had been so long since she'd seen so much of his flesh.

Her heart pounding, her throat suddenly dry, she watched his eyes flicker from hers to her mouth. *Stop this. Don't complicate everything.* She moved away quickly. That her pulse was beating faster was easy to explain. Reflex, she told herself. Nothing more. He was her husband, almost her ex. She couldn't allow herself to forget that he was only *playing* happy husband.

Luke followed her out, flicking off the light and wandering through the darkening hallway. In passing, he glanced at the bed in their bedroom. By her reaction a minute ago, he had a distinct feeling that he wasn't going to enjoy that soft mattress tonight.

Val decided the smart thing was to keep her distance from him. With the girls, she curled up on the sofa to watch a Disney movie. To her relief, when Luke came down the steps, he disappeared into his den to call Fred Henderson about patients. They wouldn't even be together now if it weren't for the twins, she reminded herself more than once while she watched the cartoon characters.

When the movie came to an end, she kissed the top of each girl's head. She'd been trying to keep close to the schedule Carrie had for them. "It's time for bed. As soon as we pick up the toys."

Traci resisted, snuggling closer. Brooke scrambled off the sofa and plopped down beside the miniature tea set. Instead of putting toys together, she pulled out another doll.

"Brooke," Val said softly. "Let's put the toys away."

Intent now on talking to her doll, Brooke shook her head as she scurried across the room to retrieve another doll. "Lu-cas do it," she said the moment she spotted him coming out of his den.

Whatever she was volunteering him for, he wasn't interested. "No, you do it," he said firmly.

In a huff, clearly feeling put upon, she plopped onto the floor. Pushing out her lower lip, she lifted each toy in the manner of an octogenarian afflicted with severe and painful arthritis.

"This is going to take all night," Luke muttered, aware now what she'd been trying to hustle him into doing for her.

Val discerned some kind of compromise was needed. "Okay, tonight we'll help."

Raising her face, Brooke rewarded her with a lip-splitting grin.

Luke sidled close. "You know what that look means," he mumbled in Val's ear. "Sucker."

The heat of his breath so close was unsettling. Val took a step away. She'd heard amusement more than criticism in his voice and relied on humor to keep the mood casual. "Speak for yourself." Smiling, she dropped to the floor with an enticement. "I bet I can put more away than either of you can," she said to both of the girls.

Traci shook her head. "Uh-uh."

"Bet I can."

"Me can." Brooke scooped up several blocks and let them clamor to the bottom of the box. Across from her, Traci raced to grab some.

Val did her best not to look too smug.

Half an hour later the twins were bathed and dressed in pajamas. Timing was everything, Val believed. If she waited too long, they might get their second wind. After urging them into bed, she started reading the books they'd chosen. With the sound of Traci's yawn, Val skipped a line to speed up the story.

"No, Vali," Brooke countered, shaking her head.

Carrie had told Val the girls knew the stories word for word and wouldn't accept even a slight change in the reading. Val backed up several lines to read the story as it was written.

Retreating into themselves, their eyes grew dreamy-looking. Val finished the story, then descended the steps and motioned upward to Luke. "They're waiting for your good-night." As he passed her on the stairs, she offered advice. "Don't get conned. I already read them a book."

In the kitchen, she poured a glass of juice. Though exhausted, she snatched a book from the top of the refrigerator. As good as the story was, Val had doubts she'd make it through one chapter before falling asleep. With the book tucked under her arm and the glass of juice in her hand, she strolled from the kitchen toward the steps.

Already slouched on a chair in the living room, Luke was dawdling over a last cup of coffee.

Val detoured and dropped to the sofa. "Are the twins asleep?"

"After I read the ending of one book." As her hand fluttered across the book she'd laid in her lap, his gaze fixed on her fingers and the rings he'd slid on one of them four years ago.

"The one with the baby giraffe?"

"That's the one."

"No wonder they know it word for word." She sipped her juice. "Did the guys at the office interview anyone yet for the receptionist's job?"

"Tomorrow." The conversation didn't interest him. He wanted to know where he was sleeping tonight. "They're going to talk to Jolene Rizer. She seems like a good candidate."

Their choice pleased her. Jolene, a young, single mother, was trying to start over after a messy divorce. Val wiggled her toes in her sneakers, wishing she was already in bed. Feeling lazy and too content just sitting still, she had to force herself to a stand. She reached the stairs and looked over her shoulder to say good-night to Luke.

He hadn't moved, but he was staring at her, studying her. "Since I'm sleeping here, where am I supposed to do that?"

Another problem, Val mused. This one was monumental. They hadn't shared a bed in weeks. Even before that, contact had stopped. They definitely needed to talk—again. "It seems easier to me—well, it's best if we keep everything platonic."

A half grin cut a deep crease into his cheek. "'Platonic'?"

"Yes. I thought that was understood," she said, nervous suddenly as he stood and moved so only inches separated them.

Though he wanted to, Luke didn't pull her closer, didn't lower his head, but desire taunted him. It had been so damn long since they'd kissed. Her skin tempting him, he stroked a knuckle across her throat.

"I know this isn't an easy situation." She could barely think with his eyes, dark and restless, on her and the warmth of his breath fanning her face. As he continued to caress her, she placed a hand on his forearm to stop him and felt his muscle tense beneath her fingers. "I thought it would be best if you slept in your den," she said a little breathless and nudged his hand away.

"My den?" Luke wasn't sure if he was amused, frustrated or furious. "What about appearances' sake, that kind of stuff?"

"We're in our own home. In here, we're getting a divorce." She was amazed she was actually making sense.

"And out there," he asked, his voice quiet and smooth, almost lulling, "we're madly in love?"

Her skin warm, she struggled to remind him, "We've been married four years." *Quit looking at me like that.* "People don't expect us to act like honeymooners."

Fooling them wouldn't be hard, Luke decided. But could they fool themselves? Before he said more, Val squeezed by him to hike up the steps. For a second— a breathtaking one—she'd nearly swayed against him.

She changed clothes then tumbled into bed. Three times she shifted to find a comfortable position. Fluffing her pillow, she stretched her legs. She was overtired. That's all that was wrong. She'd kept pace with the twins, fueled by caffeine. That explained, too, why she couldn't sleep now. Why she kept imagining Luke's long legs and sturdy frame cramped on the settee in his den.

Chapter Four

On a groan, Luke eased himself upright on the settee and glanced toward the French windows in his den. No light. Not even the hint of dawn. Yawning, he didn't consider sleep. A foot too short for him, the settee had already gotten the best of him. Standing, he yanked on his jeans, buttoning them as he ambled out of the den.

Before he padded up the dark stairway to the bathroom, he called his service. A message from Fred Henderson about him having an emergency meant telling Val that they'd have to postpone moving the furniture out of his den until later.

Upstairs, he opened the bathroom door and stumbled. Cursing, he hit the light switch and stared down at potty chairs. Not a minute passed when he wasn't aware of how much Val's and his life had changed almost overnight.

When he'd contemplated being a father, he'd imagined a gradual change in his life-style. He'd expected midnight feedings and constant diaper changes, not chattering toddlers.

With nothing else to do at five-thirty in the morning, he climbed into the shower and let steaming water run over his skin. Muscles aching from his night on the short sofa welcomed the warmth.

Physically, he felt better when he opened the shower door, stepped out and snatched a towel from the rack. But he stared in the mirror at a man he sometimes didn't recognize. Though he'd worked hard most of his life, he'd never felt defeated by anything. The guy staring back at him looked like a quitter. He'd given up something that Luke had thought would never slip from his grasp, the woman he loved.

It had come as a surprise to realize that love sometimes wasn't enough. "Love conquers all" equated to a lot of mumbo jumbo. Who knew better than he that two people could love and still lose?

He yanked on the clean briefs and jeans that he'd left in the bathroom last night, then lathered shaving cream onto his face. Every day, he shaved. For Val, even when they'd gone camping, he'd performed the task daily because during a nuzzle or a kiss, the short stubble of his beard reddened her face. He paused in spreading the cream on his jaw. He hadn't been that close to her in months. So why was he doing this?

Turning on the water, he held his razor under the spigot for a second. As the water flowed into the sink, the door flung open.

"Whatcha doin'?" In a yellow robe and puppy-faced slippers, Brooke tipped her head, following his movement with the razor.

"Morning, kiddo."

"Lu-cas up."

Another adjustment. No privacy, he realized. Tomorrow he'd remember to lock the bathroom door. He swiped the razor down his cheek, then complied to her request.

As she stood on the closed toilet seat, she viewed herself in the mirror. Thoughtfully she studied his movement while he dragged the razor down his jaw. "Me can do," she said, and imitated the motion with her toothbrush.

Luke played along and dabbed shaving cream on her chin and on each pudgy cheek. "Where's Traci?"

"Dressin'." Her lips spread into a grin, her eyes twinkling above the smudge of shaving cream he'd also put on the tip of her nose. "Look, Vali." Delight danced in her voice. "Me shabin'."

In the doorway, Val smiled back at her, but her attention strayed to a rivulet at the base of Luke's throat. It streamed down the smooth, flowing muscular flesh. Crystal droplets beaded the dark hair on his head. She smelled the soap on him, the cleanness. Amazingly she somehow managed not to take a more leisurely look.

Luke knew if he'd taken another downstroke with the razor, he'd have cut himself for sure.

Finally listening to a command from her brain to move, Val backed into the hallway and held out a hand to Brooke. "You need to get dressed."

Before Brooke tumbled off the toilet lid, Luke lowered her to the floor.

"Me go find Traci?"

"Yes," Val urged. *And I need to get out of here.*

Alone again, Luke waited a long moment to steady himself before he resumed shaving. Things weren't much clearer between them except—except last night he'd felt the pulse at her throat thudding when he'd touched her. And seconds ago he'd have sworn he'd seen *that* look in Val's eyes, a warm softness that had always preceded a caress, a kiss, a subtle brushing of her body against his.

Standing at the stove, Val dropped pancake batter on a sizzling skillet. Being honest with herself and her own feelings had always come easily to her. Pleasure. Pure pleasure had rippled through her minutes ago. But so what? she countered. All that meant was hormones were still on track. With the ring of the phone, she lowered the heat on the burner, then offered a greeting.

In her usual bubbly manner, Jenny filled her in on what the swooning gossip triplets, good friends and town busybodies, Agnes, Minny and Ethel, were aghast about now.

"It doesn't take much to shock them," Val said lightly over the loud giggling of the twins as they made up words to the delight of each other.

"How are your first days of motherhood going?"

Val flipped pancakes onto plates. "Mind-boggling."

"If you need help, I could come over," Jenny offered.

Wedging the receiver between her jaw and shoulder, Val cut the pancakes, then set them in front of the twins. "Thanks, but I'm sure Gramps and Irene will both do their share of doting over them."

"And Luke?"

It was hard for her to keep anything from Jenny. "He's acting funny."

"Funny ha-ha? or funny strange?"

Val ran fingers sticky with maple syrup under the water. "Funny unpredictable."

"The stable, reliable Dr. Kincaid is acting unpredictable?"

Val took Jenny's words as what they were, a tease. "He's being attentive, cooperative."

"Is that so bad?"

Val wondered how to explain. Years of memories, of nights filled with his soft caresses, his seductive whispers, were spinning back at her every time she was alone with him. "He's making me nervous."

Jenny snickered. "This sounds interesting. Will you keep me informed?"

"Daily," Val promised, hanging up a second before the back door flung open.

"Well, I'm here," her grandfather gruffly announced.

"Hi, Gramps." Val twisted away from the stove for a hug. "I'll make some decaf and—"

"I don't want the unleaded stuff." He smacked a kiss on each twin's cheek, then dropped to a chair.

"Didn't your doctor tell you not to drink caffeine?"

"He told me. When you get old, doctors torture you to death with their Don't lists."

Concern and affection mingled. Gently Val nagged, "Gramps, you eat the wrong food. A man who's had a heart bypass has to watch his diet."

"Don't like them phony eggs."

As he sent her a scowl, Val wondered if she was wasting her breath. Her endearingly crotchety grandfather usually did as he pleased. Unfortunately he had a propensity for high fat and high cholesterol foods.

"Reached seventy-one doing whatever I damn well please. Don't need any female nagging me about what I should and shouldn't do." His gaze shifted to a favorite wall plaque of his late wife's. "Your grandmother always liked that, too."

Val remembered. As a young girl visiting her grandparents, she'd been fascinated by the bright yellow plaque shaped like a teakettle that hung on a wall in their kitchen. When her grandmother had died, she'd wanted nothing of hers except that plaque.

Tenderness seeped into her grandfather's voice. "Glad you took it."

Val returned his smile, aware he'd gotten rid of almost none of her grandmother's possessions.

"Only one I'll ever love," he mumbled. "About time all the dang females in this town wake up to that."

That he was grumbling with his usual complaint about being pursued by too many women didn't surprise Val. "That's what you get for being *the* biggest catch in town," she teased.

"Don't know why they're after an old goat like me. Goes to show you, they lose all good sense after turning seventy."

"Who's after you now?" Val asked while wiping the twins' sticky fingers.

"Beatrice Elwood. Been dodging her for days. The last time she trapped me to have lunch with her, she made me a fruit salad. That's no lunch for a man. This town needs more eligible bachelors. Old geezers like me."

Val rolled her eyes then lowered the twins from their highchairs. "You try to make sense with him," she said to Luke as he came into the kitchen carrying the morning newspaper. "I have to get the twins' shoes."

His head swiveling around to follow her movement from the room, Edwin barely waited until she'd disappeared with the girls. "Have you thought over what we talked about, Luke?"

Luke needed no further explanation. Romance was on the old man's mind. "She wants the divorce, Edwin."

"Has she seen Harry yet?" he asked, referring to their lawyer.

Luke didn't try to explain. Before either of them had made that appointment, the girls had entered their lives. But there was nothing he could say that would be any different now than it had been when Edwin had first guessed that they'd discreetly separated.

"Luke, you know what family means to her. Her mother taught her well. Valerie watched her flit from one man to the next. Divorced three times," he said, shaking his head as if that had happened yesterday instead of decades ago. Luke knew the story, but the old man seemed compelled to remind him. "Valerie never knew any real home life, never could depend on having any father for very long. Only the brief summers she spent with her grandmother and me ever gave her a sense of home and family. She always said she'd marry only once. That isn't a woman who believes in divorce.''

Val hadn't meant to eavesdrop, but a step from the kitchen doorway, she heard her grandfather's rambling. ''Gramps, stop. Right now,'' Val insisted.

''From everything I'm hearing, this is nothing more than a bogus marriage. For how long?'' he challenged.

That question couldn't be answered. Ignoring it, Val cleared dishes off the twins' highchairs. ''Luke and I made an agreement,'' she said, moving to the doorway and checking on the girls playing with blocks in the living room.

Her grandfather's dark eyes darted from her to Luke and zeroed in on her again. ''A friendly one?''

His stern stare had always made her fidget. She fought the urge to do so now. She was thirty-two, not twelve. Grabbing a dishtowel, she began drying a glass that had been draining in the sink rack.

''Well, is it?'' he insisted.

Val faced him squarely. ''Of course.''

In what could only be interpreted as disgust, he snorted and started for the back door. ''Married people can't be only friends. It isn't natural.''

Val looked to Luke for reinforcement. He merely shrugged. ''Gramps, we have to convince the court. We have to give the impression of having a solid marriage.''

''What you both need is a good swift kick in the backside,'' he muttered.

At a loss for words, Val laughed as he shut the door behind him. "He does like to have his say." She grabbed a sponge and wiped off the highchair trays. "What are you going to move out of the den?"

"Everything but the desk." Luke ran a hand over the back of his neck. "I'll have to do it later. Fred left a message for me. He had an emergency, so I have to go in to the office." After saying he'd be there to help, that he was leaving her to deal with things didn't sit well with him. He disappeared into the living room to kiss the girls goodbye. Stepping back into the kitchen he started for the door but stopped. He couldn't go yet. One question had gnawed at him through every quiet moment he'd had last night. "Val, this isn't too hard on you, is it?"

All women knew motherhood wasn't a cinch. "Well, they are exhausting, but adorable."

Luke considered letting her answer satisfy him, but he couldn't take the easy way out. "That's not what I meant."

All she had to do was look at him. A remoteness had swept into his eyes. He was thinking about their daughter. It seemed odd to her that they'd mentioned Kelly more in the past twenty-four hours than they had in seven months. "I want the twins. My feelings for them have nothing to do with Kelly," she said, sensing what he wasn't saying.

Luke couldn't back off. "You said no more children."

How could she explain? What hadn't made sense to her before suddenly did. Why? she wondered. Because she was finally healing? "When you suggested having another child, I wasn't ready." Did he understand? How would she know? Whatever his feelings were, he'd keep them to himself. The connection so vivid and so natural between them had disappeared. With his silence, a new worry sprang up within her. "You don't want them?"

"Did I say that?"

No, you tell me nothing, she wanted to say.

"I made a promise, too. Do you think so little of me that you don't think I'd keep it?" He didn't wait for an answer but walked out the door. It was clear how little faith she had in him. But could he blame her? She'd been alone in the delivery, alone when she'd been told how ill their newborn daughter was. If he'd been with her then, everything might have been different. No, that wasn't true.

On that February night, he'd stepped out of surgery and learned he'd become a father, but his daughter was dying. He'd rushed to Val's room but by then she'd been so distraught she'd barely looked at him as they'd waited. Their baby had died, and there'd been nothing Luke could have done. He couldn't have changed the final outcome, but that knowledge didn't ease the burden he carried with him since that night.

Val stood at the kitchen door for only a second, then rushed outside. His back to her, he was slipping the key in the car door. She couldn't let him leave this way. Deeply she breathed and braced herself, not for more anger but for what hurt the most—no reaction. "Luke, I'm sorry."

God, don't say that. Those were his words, the ones he'd never been able to say.

"I really want them," Val went on. "And—I'm afraid."

The ache, identifiable now, rose up within him.

"None of this is easy." Val stared at his broad back. There was a time when she'd wanted to see his eyes so she'd know his mood. Now it didn't matter. Even when she stared into them, he was a mystery to her. "Couldn't we have a truce?" As he turned around, she held his gaze despite a cowardly shiver that urged her to retreat. "Couldn't we?"

Luke wasn't sure how to handle the moment. He wanted to pull her into his arms. He wanted to give her assurances. The slip of a smile she delivered made him feel like hell. With his nod, she turned away. *I'll do right by you this time.* He kept the words to himself, but it was a promise he planned to keep.

Val had nudged herself to move. No matter what she did or how hard she tried, he still slammed a door in her face, and she didn't know why.

With a frustrated sigh, she entered the house to giggles and the theme song for "Sesame Street." She set a cup of milk for each twin on the coffee table. With them content and glued to the antics of Big Bird and Cookie Monster, she returned to the kitchen.

Leaving the back door open allowed a breeze to cool the kitchen. She flicked on the radio, turned the volume low and began wiping smudges from little fingers off the refrigerator.

"Valerie?" a feminine voice called.

Val spun around. She peered at the face obscured by the screen door for only a second before she identified the visitor. It took another second, a long one, for her to find the politeness she'd been raised to extend to company. It didn't really matter.

The woman didn't wait for an invitation. She opened the screen door and stepped into the kitchen. "I'm sure you know who I am."

She did and was suddenly uneasy. A tingling slithered over the back of Val's neck. The kind of tingle she got when watching a horror movie where, as the dumb heroine inched down the stairs to the dark basement, Val just knew that the psycho killer was waiting for her.

Tall, shapely and blond, with heavily shadowed eyes, this woman hardly fit that description. Her major offense centered on her bad taste in clothes. In her forties, she wore a thigh-length leather skirt and a hot pink, knit top that was one size too small. Since Val had arrived in New Hope, she'd spoken to Charlene Dawson Evans no more than half a dozen times. Joe Dawson's cousin socialized in a different circle of friends, so they'd had nothing in common—until now.

"The twins are here, aren't they?"

The screen door closed behind Charlene. "Yes, your cousins are."

"Actually I think of them as my nieces." She slid the strap of her beaded purse off her shoulder and stepped further into the kitchen, looking around it like a prospective buyer inspecting a house for defects.

"Who's she?" Wide-eyed, Traci came into the kitchen, cradling her cup in her hands.

A protective instinct rose within Val to block Charlene's path as she sauntered toward Traci.

Charlene's voice sang with sweetness. "I'm your cousin, Charlene. Are you Traci or Brooke?"

Funny, Val thought, but she'd never had trouble identifying them.

"Traci." She leaned close to Brooke, now standing beside her.

Charlene patted her head. "Oh, aren't you both cute. You can call me Auntie Charlene."

The girls weren't receptive to a stranger. And that's what Charlene was to them. They'd never met her. She hadn't been at the hospital when Carrie had the girls. She hadn't gone to the church for their baptism. She'd never sent a birthday present or a Christmas gift. She didn't know anything about them except their names.

Brooke reacted predictably, pulling back and scurrying to Val to hide behind her leg.

Charlene excused her reluctance with what she wanted to see. "Shy little thing, isn't she?"

Traci gazed up at Val for some kind of confirmation about the woman reaching out to touch her, then suddenly lunged for Val's other leg.

Val said the obvious. "They don't know you, Charlene."

She spared Val a glance. "Well, we'll soon change all that."

Val recognized the worst of her fears since Charlene had arrived becoming a possibility. "What do you mean?"

"They're my cousin's children. Who do you think they should be with? A stranger or a blood relative?"

Protectively, Val draped a hand over each girl's shoulder, pulling them tighter to her. If she believed Charlene really wanted them, she'd be more understanding. But Charlene hadn't even been at Joe and Carrie's funeral. "You're the stranger."

Charlene's smile turned deadly on Val, then she cast a quick glance at the girls. "You'll get used to Auntie Charlene," she assured them.

Her meaning was clear.

"We'll be seeing each other again, Valerie."

When the screen door slammed shut behind her, Val dropped to her knees to hug the girls. She'd heard the vague threat in Charlene's words. Fear pumping through her, she took several deep breaths, worried she'd frighten the twins if she didn't calm down.

"Bad lady?" Brooke asked.

Val fought the urge to say yes. "No, sweetheart. She's not a bad lady."

"Me no like."

Traci shook her head. "Traci no like."

Don't panic, Val told herself. She and Luke were the twins' godparents, were chosen by Joe and Carrie to raise their daughters.

"Vali?"

Hearing the distress in Traci's voice, Val forced a smile and nuzzled her neck. "Where did you get that mustache?" she teased at the milk outlining the little one's lips.

With Traci's grin, Val kissed her, then hugged both of them longer than they might have liked.

"Can I get one of those, too?"

Both girls swung grins toward Irene standing at the back door, her arms open to them.

They dashed to her with their tale. "Bad lady," Traci insisted with an arm curled around Irene's neck. Nestled on the other side of her, Brooke nodded her head in confirmation.

Not wanting them to dwell on the visit, Val directed them back toward the television. The graham cracker she gave them worked wonders at distracting them from more thoughts about Charlene.

Val expected Irene to pounce on her the moment she returned to the kitchen. What she wasn't prepared for was Luke's scowl.

"Who scared them?" he asked, indicating his mother had told him about the girls' reaction to a visitor.

"Yes, who's the bad lady?" Irene said heatedly. "The woman doing the home study?"

"We haven't seen her yet," Val answered. Puzzled, she looked at Luke. "I thought you were going to the office."

"I changed my mind." One call on his cellular phone to another colleague had handled that situation. He wanted to know about this one. "Who the hell scared them?" he asked impatiently.

"Charlene Dawson," Val said, a lot steadier than she felt.

Irene gasped, indicating imagined fears had popped into her mind.

Only one thing mattered in Luke's mind. "What did she say?"

It didn't help that he sounded anxious. She had to be mistaken. Luke was described by everyone as a man to have around during a moment of crisis. She couldn't even recall a lapse in that strength when Kelly had died. Stalwart, unwavering, he'd revealed toughness and courage. The strong, silent type, people had murmured about him after the funeral. Trying to quiet nerves, she poured them coffee and relayed what had transpired during Charlene's visit.

"Like hell she will." Luke wanted the twins. Even two years ago when Joe had approached him about naming him and Val guardians, if ever needed, Luke had felt no hesitation.

"That's absurd." Irene held her spoon but didn't stir the sugar she'd dropped into her cup. "She has no legal rights to them."

Val drew a hard breath. God, she hoped she was worrying unnecessarily. She prayed that was true.

Irene finished stirring the sugar in her coffee. "It would have been better if you'd been home, Lucas."

Luke said nothing. What was the point? Again, he hadn't been near when Val had needed him.

As the girls popped into the room for another graham cracker, Val told them no. "You can have a banana."

"I'll get it." Irene reached for the fruit bowl. "Valerie, don't worry," she said, peeling the banana and splitting it for the girls.

But she would, Luke knew. She would smile for others and fret every minute that she was alone. With a glance at the clock, he started for the door. He didn't plan to leave anything to chance this time. It was enough that Val had lost one child. If she had to lose two more.... He shoved the thought aside, unwilling to consider the possibility.

"Where are you going?" The question came out in unison from both women.

"To see Harry," he called back from the door. "We're not losing them."

"Oh, dear." Irene sat unbelievably still. "He wouldn't see a lawyer if he wasn't worried."

And now she was, too, Val discerned, because Luke had shown an inkling of uneasiness about Charlene's intentions. From the time her husband had died, Irene had depended on Luke's calm strength and confident optimism during crises. Val offered words meant to soothe. "He believes in prevention, remember?" she said lightly.

Irene managed a weak smile. "Oh, yes, that's right. But what if..."

"No, we're not going to do that," Val insisted to ease Irene's anxiousness.

For the next ten minutes Val directed their conversation toward the big wedding of the year between Michael Russo and Michelle Parker.

"It should be lovely," Irene agreed, finishing her coffee. "Do you want me to stay until Luke returns?"

"No, I'm fine." Val repeated three times before Irene backed out of the driveway. Of course, she wasn't. All her certainty slithered away like a retreating snake. In dire need of activity to keep from thinking about Charlene's words, she took the girls outside to the sandbox, and helped them make cakes of sand. There were a dozen other things she could be doing. At the moment, though, she needed to be with them.

After a light lunch and naptime, Val and the twins fingerpainted and had a tea party. They had an early dinner, then Val gave them their baths, which they finished before Luke arrived home.

"Harry was in Dallas. I waited for him," he said in explanation for his lateness. "What's her problem?"

he asked about Traci. On the floor, she stared into space as if thinking hard. By her downturned mouth, wrinkled brow and pushed-out lower lip, she gave the impression nothing was right in the world.

Though Brooke had shoveled in her share of dinner, Traci had merely picked at the meal. "She wanted pizza."

"Persistent. Didn't she want it for breakfast, too?"

Nodding, Val drummed up a smile. "I didn't know how late you'd be, but I kept dinner warm for you."

"Thanks." He noted the broccoli cheese soup and the stuffed pork chops, both favorites of his.

Though anxious to know what Harry had said, Val deliberately didn't ask, deciding to wait until after she'd tucked the girls into bed.

Alone in the kitchen, Luke read the evening newspaper while he ate dinner. He finished as the girls came in and delivered good-night kisses. The silence around him, the aloneness, had never bothered him before. Because of emergencies, he'd often found himself eating late at night after Val had gone to bed. But now was different. He was getting used to giggles and noise and spills.

Washing up his dish and silverware, he sensed the ties binding him and Val and the twins. Though they'd been together only a short time, they were becoming a part of each other—a family.

Picking up his coffee, he strolled into his den and gave the room a once-over. He needed to move another table and small bookcase. A floor lamp that was likely to topple on one of the girls had to go, too.

"What did Harry say?" Val asked the moment she entered the room.

Luke heard a trace of anxiety in her voice. "He'll work to get the court hearing scheduled as soon as possible."

Can Charlene get them? Val struggled against that one thought. "What did he say about Charlene?" she asked instead.

"He thought he'd have heard about her intentions if she was serious."

Her veiled threat hadn't sounded flippant to Val. But she knew now that she had to believe the girls were with them for good. Whatever she did, she couldn't let doubts grab hold.

Looking to keep busy, she made a mental list—more storage space for toys, paint for the walls and bright-colored fabric for curtains. Bending over the toy box, she strained to push it across the floor to a corner.

"I'll do that." Lifting the toy box, Luke glanced sideways at her. She actually looked calm to him. "Where do you want this?"

"Over there." Val indicated a corner.

"I noticed earlier the clothes hanging on door-knobs." He snatched up the lamp. "If you need more closet space, I could get one of those wardrobe units from the hardware store."

Like her, he'd obviously decided to focus energy on getting the girls settled in so they felt this was their home. "Actually, I found a place for the extra clothes." Val decided not to tell him what he learned soon enough when he opened his bulging closet.

As he left for the garage, Val rounded the desk to answer the phone. With most of the furniture in the garage, the girls should have plenty of space for playing. That was the last coherent thought Val believed she had. She listened to the caller and thought she returned polite responses that made sense. She knew that she'd kept her voice steady, but before she ended the call, she'd braced her legs against the arm of the sofa.

So much was happening at once. Sensing Luke's return, she raised her gaze from the carpet. "The phone call was from a home study worker." She'd been honest with him before about the twins. She was scared even before Charlene had dropped her bombshell. So much depended on them making the right impression. "We're going to be checked out."

Luke caught the quick flash of distress in her face before she turned away to stare out the window.

Val battled demons of uncertainty. Looking up, she saw the night sky was clouded with the promise of rain. It seemed as if so much was unpredictable in their lives suddenly.

Vulnerable. She looked so vulnerable that Luke wanted to take her into his arms. Instead he crossed to the settee, leaving her alone with her thoughts. Though he'd kept himself in shape lifting weights, he'd need an extra pair of arms to carry the settee to the garage.

"I'll help," Val said, sidestepping dollhouse furniture. She weaved a path around a stuffed lion and a white fluffy bunny to take a position on the opposite side of the settee. "It might be a problem for us to pull off this charade in front of someone so experienced at seeing through people," she said as they negotiated their way through the doorway. With a little maneuvering around corners, they set the settee down in the garage.

His brows bunched with a frown. "We might have another problem."

Val preceded him into the kitchen. "What problem?" With his silence, she stopped and looked back. He was so near that he plowed into her. Her head jerked up as he pulled her close. Unsure if he'd grabbed her intentionally or to steady her, she gave him a quick, strained laugh. Whatever the reason, a longing rose within her as he lightly fingered the short strands of her hair. "What problem?" she barely managed to ask again.

He couldn't let her go. In a slow, seductive move, Luke ran his other hand down her spine. Against his chest, her heartbeat quickened. Closer to her than he'd been in months, he felt need spike through him. "I no longer have a bed," he said, bringing his mouth a hairbreadth from hers. "You know what that means."

She knew that lovemaking would *really* complicate everything. "It means that you sleep on the sofa in the living room," she countered, a touch breathless.

"Think again," he said with steely softness.

When his eyes flicked to her mouth, all the warnings she'd give herself later eluded her. With a hand at the back of her neck, he held her still. The instant his mouth closed over hers, she felt all the excitement again. No man except him had ever made her feel so much, so quickly. She hadn't forgotten his taste or the feel of his arms around her. Though the kiss was gentle, the pressure proved deep enough to spring alive everything that had been buried within her for months.

A soft moan escaped from her throat. He wasn't just any man. He was the one she'd pledged to love forever. And with one kiss, she tasted a promise and a demand for what had been. Time ticked away somewhere, but for her, it stopped. An ache gnawed at her that was familiar, too familiar. As his mouth twisted across hers, she tried to reason. Instead she savored.

Feelings swarmed her. Sensation rose and intensified. Her senses heightened as she floated on the scent of his after-shave, obeyed the play of his tongue, seducing and inviting her own.

As if measuring them, she moved her hands across his shoulders. Muscles shifted beneath his shirt, and she remembered all that had been. Everything was with her again, even the yearning for him, for the texture of his damp skin beneath her touch.

Luke hadn't been sure how she'd react—fire or ice. He only knew he needed her taste. It was sweet, so damn sweet. And the heat of her willing mouth was more than he'd expected. He caught her tighter to him as memories flooded him of an intimate moment, of her face cast in the moonlight when she'd leaned close to him, of her warmth engulfing him, of her sighs and whispered words of love. He'd known her love, couldn't forget the tenderness or the heat of it. It was burned into his memory just as his need for her was burrowed so deeply into him that he knew no other woman would ever touch him in quite the same way.

He hadn't known how much he longed for her, or how hard it would be to let her go. Pulling back, he was pleased to see her eyes barely opened, to feel her fingers tight on his arms. "I'm sleeping in our bed."

Her breath ragged, Val fought for steadiness. He'd spoken with such quietness that she knew he'd meant it. "Fine." She struggled to look in control. Was that possible with her face flushed and her lips swollen from his kiss? "You stay on your side of the bed, and I'll stay on mine."

The urge to crush her to him was too fierce. Luke stepped back. She'd made it sound so simple.

He already knew that it wouldn't work for him.

Chapter Five

Of course it didn't work.

A shift of her leg under the sheet, and Val brushed against his. "You're on my side."

His back to her, Luke sensed a long night ahead of them. "I'm bigger."

Miffed about a situation she knew could get out of hand, she turned her back on him and wiggled closer to the edge of the mattress. "You're hogging the sheet," she said, unable to shed a testy mood.

Besides the irritation in her voice, he heard her punch her pillow. "You're going to fall off the bed."

"I won't." But it was impossible to find a comfortable spot. *That* could only be found in the middle of the bed. And she wasn't going there. Trying to curl deeper in the covers, she gave a hard yank on them. "Will you give me some of the sheet?"

Luke released his grip on it and the light comforter, lifting his hands in the air. With her one swift pull, what remained on him was enough to cover his one leg and arm. In the darkness, he stared at the back of her head. "Don't snore," he said to rile her more because he was bothered, in a different way, with her sweet scent teasing him.

An indignant tone that would have done a princess proud edged her voice. "I don't. You do."

"Never."

"Always. Oh, go to sleep." Val clamped her lips shut, clung to the mattress and closed her eyes. A long time passed before she went to sleep.

By morning they were rump to rump. Eyes closed, she felt him stir, sprawling. For a second, his arm pressed into the small spot between her shoulder blades. Then, in a gesture so familiar she ached with the memories it aroused, he turned, draping a taut muscular arm around her waist and a strong leg over hers. Val listened to his steady, even breaths of sleep, felt them caressing the nape of her neck.

Keeping her eyes shut, she lay perfectly still, too aware of the hand resting beneath the curve of her breast. Softly he snored, and for a moment, one that was longer than wise, she remained in his embrace with his face buried in the curve of her neck.

Staring down at the arm on her, with a fingertip she grazed the soft, dark hair on his forearm. How easy it would be to stay in his arms, to snuggle into him, to trace the flat, hard plane of his stomach. And what a mistake that might be. Nothing had changed. Intimacy and closeness weren't synonymous.

So he'd kissed her, and he'd smiled a few times. He still hadn't let her past the wall he'd erected since Kelly died. In slow motion to not wake him, she inched to the edge of the mattress. Thank God, he was still asleep.

Luke opened one eye. Instead of something soft and lacy, she wore a sleep shirt with Garfield on the front of it. The heavier cloth didn't stop him from visualizing the softness of her breasts, the angles of her hips, the slimness of her legs. They were burned in his memory.

Now feet from the bed, she snatched up her robe. Silently he cursed and turned his face into her pillow. Her scent washed over him. One kiss had reminded him of the first one. He'd never known such obsession for any woman's taste before—so much need for another person.

Intelligent, caring, sensitive, she had distracted him from everything in a way no one else could. She eased his mind when he would come home tired and discouraged because his knowledge and medicine had failed one of his patients. She'd been all he ever wanted.

Feeling sixteen and frustrated again, he pushed himself from the bed and shimmied into his jeans. And he faced a truth. He could feed himself nonsense about accepting the divorce plans, but a slip of paper wouldn't dissolve what he felt for her.

He'd only agreed to the divorce because he hadn't known how to reach his wife, hadn't seen any future for them, wasn't sure if she might still want him. But everything was different now. The warm, loving woman he'd married was back, and he wanted her.

And one kiss had revealed that her feelings for him weren't dead.

He entered the bathroom with a reminder to lock the door. For longer than usual, he stayed under the water in the shower. It was a bunch of bull that cold showers helped calm male libidos. Nothing would help.

Over the next week, Val believed things worked well between her and Luke. Sort of. The problem stemmed from her, not him. More often than she wanted to admit, she found herself longing for the time when she could sit with him late at night to share some silly but remarkable feat one of the girls had accomplished that day.

What hadn't happened was another kiss. Though they'd slept in the same bed, and more than once she'd awakened curled against his back or with her head resting on his chest, she reminded herself that passion alone wouldn't heal the wounds.

With a late September heat wave adding to Val's discomfort, she took the twins to the community pool. Under her watchful eye, they splashed around in the kiddie pool until nearly two-thirty. Their pale blond hair shining bright beneath the sunshine, they dragged towels and meandered from the car toward the house. As Val looked up from fishing the keys from her shoulder bag, she noticed not only Luke's car in the driveway but also a white van.

Dressed in white overalls, a tall, thin man strolled from the house. "Afternoon, Mrs. Kincaid. Window seat is gone, and the drywall is up."

Val smiled instinctively at Pete Armstrong. "I didn't know you were coming today." She looked past him to see the girls squatting and following a bug's progress across the walkway to the grass.

"I called Doc Kincaid. He said he'd meet me here." He gave her a crooked grin and gestured with his thumb behind him. "He sure plays a mean piano, doesn't he?"

Val heard a bluesy version of "Heart and Soul." "Yes. Mean," she repeated, assuming that meant good. As he climbed into his truck, Val scooted the girls to the door. The bug had eluded their inquisitive hands.

When they entered the house, Luke's fingers danced down the keyboard to end the song.

"Went swimmin'," Brooke announced, dashing to him. One little finger flattened on a piano key.

Val hoped Luke would sit with the child at the piano some time to see if her interest was childish curiosity or a desire to play. "The room is done?" she asked, dropping her tote bag onto the closest chair.

"Still needs painting." Over Brooke's head, he swept a lengthy look up his wife's long tanned legs. "I have to go back to the office. Before I came home, I got some good news." He strained to think. What he wanted to do was slip his hands beneath the oversize shirt that skimmed her thighs and covered her bathing suit.

"What good news?"

Luke nearly grinned at her telltale nervous gesture as she suddenly tugged at the bottom of the shirt. "Harry called me."

Val gave him her full attention.

"The court hearing is scheduled for next week."

She'd expected the finalizing of their guardianship to take months, not a week. And since they hadn't heard from Charlene again, she'd almost convinced herself that Charlene's challenge had been a passing idle one. "That's wonderful." With a laugh, she snatched up the towels dropped by the twins.

Luke stared after her for a long moment. No reluctant smile. She'd flashed a dazzling one at him. "Are you going to the office to pick up work?"

She'd mentioned doing that, Val recalled. Before she got too far behind in her work, she did need to pick up receipts and ledger books to take home so she could play catch-up. "Yes." With the towels dangling from her fingers, she lifted her head. His warm gaze remained on her. Sensation skittered up her spine like a warning. Suddenly tense, she wanted to get away and escape what only he had ever made her feel. "Come on," she urged the girls, steering them back toward the door.

"Val?" His eyes narrowed, an unexpected gleam of amusement visible in them.

Val geared up for more reaction. "What?"

"You might want to change your clothes."

Okay, so he made her nervous. After several quick errands, within the hour Val pulled into the parking lot next to Luke's office. While unfastening the girls from their car seats, she was still making excuses for her reaction to him at the house. She hadn't expected to see him home. She'd forgotten about her promise to the doctors Luke shared offices with. She was muddled with so much to think about.

That all sounded extremely logical. So why were nerves present? And why had she been so damn flustered earlier with him staring at her? Because he hadn't acted indifferent to her, she realized. For that matter, for the past few days he hadn't been acting distant or uninterested. Not really.

Holding each twin by a hand, Val slowed her stride at the double-glass door entrance. Still feeling the need to draw a few long, deep breaths just in case she saw Luke inside, she stalled and noticed town busybodies Agnes, Minny and Ethel with their heads bent together, whispering. Val spotted the object of their attention. Her grandfather.

He stood nearly nose-to-nose with New Hope's newest librarian.

A sixtish widow with salt-and-pepper hair, she had a dimpled smile, a peaches-and-cream complexion and smiling blue eyes. No friendliness was in them at the moment. "Mr. Reardon, I realize the town council has a budget to meet. However, the library requires—"

"Impossible," he cut in. "'Who goeth a-borrowing, goeth a-sorrowing.'"

Her chin raised several inches. "Please refrain from quoting Thomas Tusser to me."

Val shifted her stance and patiently waited.

Myrna Traynor proved as feisty as he was. "We need funds for more books. That is what a library is, a place to find books."

Inching a few steps closer, Val saw her grandfather's face better. Despite the annoyance edging his voice, his eyes twinkled.

"Vali." Traci tugged on her hand.

Val decided this was not the time to say hello to Grandpa, and steered the girls toward the outside door of the doctors' offices.

Inside the waiting room with the twins, she understood why Carrie always laughingly commented that since the twins' birth she'd gone nowhere without gathering attention. A couple in the waiting room gushed at the twins, an elderly man wiggled his fingers to entertain them, and even the postal carrier delivering mail lingered to watch their play.

Standing at the counter, Val waited for Jolene to finish her phone call. The door of Neil Venmon's office opened, and Val prepared for a lengthy lecture about flossing.

Instead of the balding dentist, Neil's wife Cindy strolled out. A thirty-something plump blond, she bubbled, touching Traci's blond head. "Oh, they are so adorable."

Angelically, Traci grinned up at Cindy.

"I noticed that you don't dress them alike," Cindy said about the obvious.

Val hesitated until Traci wandered over to the toy box in a corner. "Carrie never did. She wanted them to be their own person."

"Carrie couldn't have chosen anyone better than you and Lucas." To emphasize her approval, Cindy squeezed her arm.

"I second that," a familiar voice said from behind them. Beaming since Mitch McCord had entered her life, Jenny offered a smile that punctuated her happiness.

"What are you doing here?" Val asked lightly, certain if Jenny had had an appointment with Luke she'd have mentioned a medical problem during their recent phone conversation.

Jenny bared her teeth in a semblance of a smile. "Had my teeth cleaned. Are they white?"

"Blinding," Val teased.

Cindy laughed along with them. "I already talked to Jenny about her and Mitch coming to our annual October party on Saturday night. You received your invitation, didn't you?"

A month ago. Val had wondered then how to refuse. They couldn't go. It was one thing to give the impression of happily married from afar, but to be so near friends for hours might require more of an acting job than she and Luke were prepared for. "I meant to call you—"

"Oh, if your problem is a baby-sitter, I wouldn't worry," Cindy cut in. "Irene is raving about the twins to everyone she sees. I'm sure she'll be delighted to sit with them for a few hours."

The sound of another door opening gave Val a moment's reprieve. Feeling as if the walls were closing in on her, she saw Luke and blessed his timing. He'd help her dodge this.

"Lucas, tell Valerie that you two will come to our party on Saturday night," Cindy persisted in one breath.

Val shifted her stance to catch his attention.

As if she were invisible, he smiled at Cindy. "What's the party for?"

"My usual October party. The kids are back in school." Cindy laughed with the private amusement of a mother of four. "So, will you come?"

Val's silent plea to say no went unnoticed. Or ignored? she wondered, narrowing her eyes at Luke.

"I don't see why not. I'm sure my mother will babysit," he said helpfully. *Too helpfully.*

"That's exactly what I told Valerie." Pleased, Cindy turned away. "So we'll expect you two," Cindy practically chirped with a wave back at them. "See you Saturday."

"Wait for me. I have to go, too," Jenny piped in, seeming awfully eager to leave.

Coward, Val mouthed when Jenny cast a look back at her. Val didn't miss her friend's grin. Plastering a sweet smile of her own on her face, she directed it to Jolene. "Does my husband have a moment or two between appointments?"

"Oh, sure, go ahead in, Valerie. I'll watch the twins," she volunteered, already skirting her desk to be near them. In a far corner, Brooke was zooming a toy truck up and down a chair leg while Traci was tugging apart toy beads meant for a one-year-old.

"Thank you." Her smile never wavering, Val stormed past Luke into his office and waited only until he'd closed the door. "We *need* to talk. What is wrong with you? Do you realize how difficult Saturday night might be?" she said in a hushed voice to keep the conversation private.

He'd forgotten the passion that danced in her eyes when she was riled. "The more people who can testify that we're a loving couple, the more the court will believe it," he said easily.

His logic abated her annoyance immediately. He was right, of course. "Luke, it's not going to be easy," she reminded him. "These people know us."

"Then we'll have to be convincing." He noted that she looked doubtful.

Outside the window, Val saw her grandfather and Myrna still bickering. "Have you met the new librarian?"

Luke skimmed his appointment book for the next one. He had five minutes before the harried manager of the New Hope Hotel came in about a stomach problem that Luke sensed might be more acid indigestion than an ulcer. "I've met her."

Less tense, Val strolled back to his desk. "By the sparks that are flying between Gramps and her, I think they have more of an attraction than an aversion to each other."

"That's hard to believe. How many times has he said that your grandmother was the only woman he'll ever love?"

"People change their minds." Val bent over and fingered the candy wrapper in his wastebasket. "Better hide these or your secret as a junk food addict will be out."

With a grin, he balled a sheet of paper and aimed it to fall strategically on top of the wrappers. "We're talking about Edwin now," he said, and perched on the front edge of his desk. "He was the most stubborn patient New Hope General ever had."

As if it were yesterday instead of five years ago, Val recalled the trouble the hospital staff had with her grandfather. "I was so scared that day." She'd taken the first flight out of Houston when she received word that her beloved grandfather had chest pains. When she rushed into New Hope General, she'd been met by her grandfather's doctor, Lucas Kincaid.

"You should have known he'd battle his way back."

Val sat beside him. What she'd known was that Luke's compassion and his assurances after her grandfather's emergency heart bypass had quieted her fear.

"What's going through your mind?"

Sitting practically shoulder to shoulder with him, she spoke honestly. "I was remembering you."

"Me?" His gaze drifted to her lips. "What about me?"

She'd been taken with him from the first meeting. It was the blue operating room scrubs, she reflected. They'd made his eyes look bluer. "I think all surgeons wear blue to calm the patient's relatives."

"Did it calm you?" he asked, toying with her gold hoop earring.

No, her heart had raced then, too. She'd have preferred to believe that it had been natural anxiety. After all, she'd been worried about her grandfather. But she remembered those moments clearly. Luke had made her heart pound as if it might burst through her chest. "You'd already told me that he'd be all right," she answered. "I believed you."

His breath fluttered across her face. "Just like that?"

"Just like that." She spoke quickly, breathing softly.

Like a butterfly's caress, he brushed a finger down the side of her neck. "For me, it was love at first sight."

A nervous wariness slipped over her. Why had she forgotten that he had a knack for surprising her? "You never told me that before."

"I didn't want you to be smug." Her soft laugh rippled over him, its low, husky tone one he'd heard often when they stood in the shower, when her eyes had danced with her playful smile, when the moisture on her skin had beckoned his lips. Edwin had assessed their situation accurately. Two people who'd been intimate couldn't pretend to be only friends.

"Still, I'm surprised," Val said, a little unsettled again as he toyed with a strand of hair near her ear.

He breathed in the scent of her, taunting himself. "About what?"

She tried to think. He wasn't making it easy. With a palm planted on his desk, he leaned closer. "I've always been more of a romantic than you," she blurted.

"I feel insulted." A smile hovering at the corners of his mouth, he framed her face with his other hand. And he took a chance. Gently he pressed his lips to her eyelid, to her cheek. "Didn't I carry you over the threshold? Didn't I throw tulip petals all over the bed?"

Val floated with him, closing her eyes when his mouth roamed to her jaw, then to the sensitive skin below her earlobe.

"You taste wonderful," he murmured, nipping at the corner of her mouth.

Unhurried, the kiss beckoned with its tenderness. She wrestled with herself to ignore the excitement pounding through her body. How could she, with his palms framing her face, with his mouth on hers? All the denials seemed useless. She was beginning to truly feel again. As he'd done when they first met, he detonated something inside her. She tasted the heat, felt it—yearned for it.

Letting the past and present tumble together, she knew she was treasuring everything far longer than she should have, far longer than was wise.

Seconds passed before a knock on the door penetrated the dreamy cloud she was drifting along on. She opened her eyes and saw his smile—and more. There wasn't the coolness that had kept her at a distance for months or the warmth that had always reflected easy amusement. In his eyes, she saw longing and determination.

With some reluctance, Luke lifted his hands from her face, but ignored the rap for another moment, absorbing the sweetness of her taste. That she'd trembled pleased him. The sweet womanly taste of her still on his lips, he pulled back. "What is it, Jolene?" he asked in a voice sounding far more in control than he felt.

Opening the door, she smiled at Val first. "I'm sorry, Dr. Kincaid, but the lab is on the phone about Mr. Tentmen's blood test. And Mr. Tentmen is here."

"Thank you." Luke sent Val a thoughtful look. Was she really only with him for the girls' sake? He couldn't believe he was misreading her that much.

Nerves scrambling, Val hung on to a smile because of Jolene and slid off the desk. "I have to leave." What was happening between them? She'd thought that everything was over.

"I have emergency room duty tonight," he said to her back.

That was just as well. Nodding, she didn't look at him again—couldn't, with the warmth of his mouth lingering on hers.

Chapter Six

A clang of metal to metal instead of an alarm clock awakened Luke at six o'clock the next morning. A moment passed before he fought through the fog of sleep, before he remembered he'd slept on the sofa in his office. When his emergency room shift was ending last night, one of his patients had admitted a granddaughter for an emergency appendectomy. Surgery had ended at three in the morning. Tired, Luke had chosen the closest place to sleep away from the hospital, his office.

Instead of the pleasing sight of Val's face, he stared now at the unshaven one of the building's maintenance man.

As if glued to the floor, Arnie slouched beside the desk, holding a wastebasket in his hand. "Sorry,

Doc." He added an apologetic grimace for good measure. "Didn't mean to wake you."

Groggy, Luke sat and raked a hand through his hair. "It's all right."

"Want me to leave?"

Despite the lingering fog of sleep, Luke noticed the curious expression on the man's face. "No, go ahead and finish."

Until this morning, he'd avoided running into anyone from the cleaning crew when he slept in his office. By the man's puzzled frown, he had plenty of questions about why Luke was sleeping at the office instead of at home in bed.

Yawning, Luke shuffled to the bathroom in his back office and scraped fingers across his unshaven jaw. He'd managed three hours of sleep and looked like hell.

He splashed water at his face, then lathered it with shaving cream, and considered the consequences of this morning's encounter with Arnie. The last thing he and Val needed was gossip about their marriage being shaky. It was ironic that someone had seen him the one time he'd been sleeping in his office out of necessity instead of as an alternative.

He made a last swipe with the razor down his morning beard and dabbed a towel at his face. Since this was his private bathroom, he'd been able to leave a set of clean clothes in it for mornings like this.

Dressed, he left the bathroom to find Arnie gone. In need of coffee, he crossed the street in the direction of Sue Ellen's Diner before he returned to the hospital. Steps from the door, he made a decision that had him walking past it.

Like a man with a mission, he detoured into the florist's. He honestly couldn't recall the last time he'd brought flowers home for Val. At some time before the world that he'd thought was perfect had spun out of control, when loving and being in love had accompanied him through each day.

He drove home and entered a quiet house. He assumed she'd gone to the store with the twins. After opening and closing several cabinets, he found a vase but, not knowing where to put the flowers, he set them on the kitchen table to surprise her.

Before noon, Val zipped into the driveway with a decision to take the stroller the next time she felt like going to the store. She switched off the ignition, then unfastened her seat belt. In the back seat, the twins hummed a song from their favorite Disney movie as Val pushed the front seat forward to get them out of their car seats.

Cradling a grocery bag in each arm, she called to Traci as she darted for the front door. "Traci, we'll go in the back door this time."

As she madly raced across the grass toward the back door, Val looked back at Brooke dawdling behind her. She tried to recall Carrie out with them and how she'd handled their tendency to go in different directions. If she remembered correctly, Carrie had never gone to the store alone with the twins. Joe had always been with her. There seemed like so much to learn about raising twins. One thing Val knew already—she'd have no dull moments anymore in her life.

At some moment Brooke had dashed by her. With Traci at the door, the two were battling for possession of the doorknob. Val didn't hurry. No one was going anywhere until she unlocked the door.

A step inside, she froze. A beautiful bouquet of yellow daisies and white mums and her favorites—yellow tulips—were arranged in a vase on the table.

"Pretty." Traci reached up to touch a petal on one of the tulips.

"Yes, pretty," Val responded, the sight of the flowers weakening her more than Luke would ever guess.

Repeatedly through the next few hours, after intervening on more than the usual amount of squabbles, she glanced at the flowers to lighten her mood.

Val assumed it was just one of those afternoons. She hoped naps would help the twins' dispositions. By two o'clock, when she was ready to leave for her volunteer work at the hospital, Irene arrived to baby-sit and assured her not to worry. Val wondered if her mother-in-law would say the same later. While she adored the twins, she'd yet to be with them on a day when they were truly grouchy.

With half an hour to spare, Val had time to make one stop before she drove to the hospital. Clutching a spray of baby's breath, she knelt in front of a grave marker in the cemetery. For a long moment she stared at the small bouquet of carnations that Luke had placed in the vase.

In no hurry, she spread her wispy-looking flowers in an arrangement around the carnations. Then, as she'd done every time, she lightly stroked the etched name on the marker. The coldness of the stone always surprised her.

Months ago, day after day, she had stopped at the cemetery after work. Back then she'd thought that Luke had never gone. She'd seen the flowers, and had believed Irene had brought them. The assumption had seemed logical at the time. She'd never run into Luke at the grave. And though he'd offered hugs of comfort, what she'd needed most back then he'd kept from her—someone to cry with.

Around her, the landscaped grounds darkened as heavy pewter clouds veiled the sun. A breeze carried the smell of rain. A long time had passed since she'd questioned why she and Luke hadn't helped each other through their painful loss. Like then, she still had no answer.

Before Val reached the hospital, she suppressed the sadness that had threatened to slip over her again. At the elevator she said goodbye to an elderly patient heading for home, then stepped out of the elevator to push a magazine cart in and out of patients' rooms. Briefly she stopped to talk to one new patient. With his request for a fishing magazine, she searched different waiting rooms for fifteen minutes to find one. The hunt had been worth it, she decided, receiving a huge grin from him. She signed the cast on his leg, then hurried to the first floor to sit in the gift shop.

People strolled in and out—some buying, others simply browsing. Smiling, Val watched one new father torn with indecision between purchasing flowers or a balloon. Eventually he ambled out of the gift shop with both.

Passing him in the doorway, another volunteer came rushing in. "I'm here, Valerie." She glanced back at the man, then smiled as she rounded the counter to take Val's place. "New daddies always look so bewildered," she said on a laugh.

Val nodded agreeably before reaching under the counter for a huge plastic bag. "See you next week," she told the woman before leaving.

As she always did on these days, she lugged the bag upstairs to pediatrics. At the nurses' station, she dropped off several stuffed animals for patients. They were garage sale finds that she cleaned up so they looked like new.

"This one is really cute," one of the R.N.'s cooed about a floppy-eared dog.

"All he needed was a new eye," Val said, smiling at the beaglelike pooch.

"I know just the little girl to give him to. A patient of your husband's. It should cheer up her day."

"A new admittance?" Val asked.

"Last night."

"Is she all right?"

The nurse smiled and looked past Val. "Fine. But if you want to know more, why don't you ask her doctor?"

Dressed in a tan sports coat and jeans, Luke was heading for the elevator. As thrilled as she'd been with the flowers from him, they underlined a minor problem. For the arrangement to stay stress-free between her and Luke, they had to keep complications at bay. "Want company?" Val asked as she approached him.

He nodded. Because she'd sought him out, he expected some heavy-duty conversation about that last kiss.

"Are you done for the day?"

"Yes." Luke punched at the button on the elevator panel. He wondered at what point she'd end the inconsequential chitchit.

As the doors opened, Val stepped ahead of him into the elevator. "You stayed at the hospital?"

"I caught a couple hours of sleep in my office."

She thought he looked dead-tired. "You have a new patient, a little girl. Is she all right?"

With only three floors to go, he'd had enough. "Why don't you say what's really on your mind?" He started to jam his hands into his jeans' pockets, but she was too close to resist.

Val knew she needed to object, but she already sensed he was in charge, not her, as he ran his thumb along her jawline. "About yesterday." She stepped back until she felt the steadying firmness of the elevator wall. "I never know what to expect," she said honestly, sharing her confusion, "but too much tension between us wouldn't be good for the girls."

He stood practically on top of her. As he placed a palm on each side of her, she was trapped by more than his body. Thoughts of the last kiss, of nights that seemed an eternity ago, held her still. "You know what I'm talking about," she said on a rushed breath. "We need some rules."

An urge to smile jabbed at him. "No flowers?"

The softness in his voice swept pleasure through her. Val wondered at what point she lost the ability to stay annoyed with him. "Don't be cruel," she murmured, unable to deny the pleasure they gave her. "The flowers are beautiful."

"What then?" He watched her eyes darkening, turning almost black as tauntingly he brushed his thumb over her lips.

He'd moved even closer, and she hadn't noticed, Val realized. So much seemed so natural between them, even the feel of his touch on her face. She pressed her hands to his chest. To stop him or to slide her fingers up to his neck? She wasn't sure. For someone who'd always been so certain of her own feelings, she was bewildered. "It would simplify everything if we stop letting this happen," she managed to say as he continued that tantalizing stroke. "You know this is impossible."

"Yes, it is." He wanted her back. He wanted everything they'd lost. Everything. "We were lovers." He spoke quietly. "We still want to be."

Val released a soft sigh. He had no idea how hard it was to resist. No idea. "Oh, Luke." With her back against the elevator wall and her heart thudding hard in her chest, she considered the change in him. He was the one who relied on logic, but what he was saying to her had everything to do with emotion, and nothing to do with what made sense.

Luke couldn't pull away, not yet. Slowly he slid a hand up from her waist. Beneath his palm, her heart hammered a wild message to him. "You want it, too."

Old sensations weaved with new ones within her as he pressed a kiss as soft as a caress along the curve of her jaw. Why was she resisting what she suddenly wanted so desperately? Emotions too strong to counter pulled at her. She thought they had called it quits, and here she was with the man who'd shared the wonders of loving with her, the man she thought she'd spend the rest of her life with.

"Do you really want me to stop?"

God, no, she didn't. And that scared her. They could hurt each other all over again. Val scrambled for control, but she was as weak around him as she'd been years ago when they met. "This could only complicate everything."

He raised a hand, curling his fingertips under her chin and forcing her face up to him. "A nice complication," he said as the elevator doors swooshed open.

They had no chance to say anything else to each other. The elevator filled with people, and twice Luke was stopped by colleagues in the parking lot.

Within seconds after they pulled their cars into the driveway, the twins dashed out the door to greet them. A step behind them, Luke's mother appeared in the doorway, looking anxious. Now what? he wondered, sliding out from behind the steering wheel.

Captured by little arms wrapped around her legs, Val lovingly ran a hand over each blond head. She realized that she might never completely understand why she'd withdrawn from Luke at first, or why he'd never shared his feelings with her during the worst weeks of their lives. But they were being blessed again. "What have you two been doing?"

"Playing store," Traci volunteered.

Even before she entered the kitchen, Val visualized her cupboard emptied of canned goods.

Standing at the counter, Irene folded a dishtowel—twice—and attempted a smile that the concern in her eyes belied. "You had a phone call."

Luke heard the unmistakable anxiety edging her voice.

"That woman from the county who's doing the home study is going to call back."

Looking down at Brooke hanging onto his leg, he scooped her up into his arms. "We've been expecting to hear from her."

But why so soon? Val wondered, wishing for more time. She sensed she and Luke stood at a crossroads. What if the woman sensed that, too? She opened the cupboard where she stored canned goods. As she'd anticipated, it was practically bare.

"I'll have them bring the cans back," Irene said behind her.

Val shook her head. "No, leave them play." Though it meant more work for her, the girls were having fun. From Luke's den, she could hear their chatter.

"Forty-eleven cents," Brooke announced, obviously manning the toy cash register.

Smiling, Val closed the cupboard. "I'll be back in a minute."

Luke visually followed her until she disappeared from view. That her mood was good meant she wasn't too upset at what had happened in the elevator.

"You look awful," his mother said, grabbing his attention.

He couldn't help smiling. "Thanks, Mom." Whipping a chair around, he straddled it and rested his forearms on the back of it. "Long night."

A look that used to proceed a motherly lecture of concern settled on Irene's face. She poured him a cup of coffee, then set it in his hand. "Everything is going better for you two now, isn't it?"

Caught off guard by her question, Luke had to remind himself that she knew nothing of his estrangement with Val. "Was something wrong?"

She leveled a stare at him. "Lucas, a man and woman who have been through the kind of tragedy you and Valerie faced are bound to have some trouble. I thought—" She hesitated, then dropped to a chair close to him, leaning forward. "I thought that might be why Valerie had wanted to leave New Hope," she said, indicating she'd been giving a lot of thought to their previous conversation about the move. "It would be logical for her to want to get away from so many difficult memories, to forget. Another place might make that easier."

Somehow he maintained a blank expression to reveal nothing, but his mother's words seeped in. So did questions. Was that the reason Val had wanted to move? Not because of him, but because of the memories? Every time she walked down a street, was she remembering a day when she'd been pregnant? When she saw the hospital, did she think about that day when she'd gone into labor? Marriages hit the skids for a lot of reasons. For them, it was the disagreement about moving away, about her dissatisfaction with her life in New Hope, that had been the catalyst for ending theirs.

"Am I interrupting something?" Val asked because Luke appeared so lost in thought.

Irene lifted her head. "Nothing," she answered, checking the clock on the wall. She took a sip of her coffee to finish her cup, then rose. "I have to go."

"Already?" Val asked. Lately, except when babysitting, her mother-in-law seemed inclined to whisk in and out of their house. "Wouldn't you like a slice of pound cake or—"

"No, no." Irene raised a protesting hand. "I'm watching my weight. Mrs. Osgood and I are walking every day to shed pounds." She wrinkled her nose. "Not too successfully, I might add," she said while offering a breezy goodbye wave.

Luke continued to mentally kick himself. Damn, but he was an idiot sometimes. Why hadn't he looked beyond the obvious when Val had told him she wanted to move? There was no easy answer to that question. At least, not one he felt comfortable facing.

Viewing the contents in the refrigerator, Val frowned. Since the elevator ride with Luke, she'd felt unsettled by the truth in his words. *You want it, too.* Over and over, his words echoed in her mind. How could she deny it when she felt so much whenever he was near her?

She rubbed a hand over the back of her neck to ease tension. For the moment, she needed to think like a mother, not a woman. Dinner had to be made. She didn't mind cooking, she simply hated having to be creative and think of something different every night. She also wasn't too keen about cleanup.

"Got a problem?" Luke asked as her brows knit.

"Dinner."

This was a problem he could handle. "What if I pick up something?"

"More fast food?" Val shook her head. "My conscience wouldn't let me say yes. Tell me what you'd like, and I'll cook."

"Got a better idea."

Since the twins would be pestering soon, she was open to all suggestions.

"I'll drive into town and pick up some fried chicken and potato salad, and we'll have a picnic on the floor in front of the television set."

In need of time to clear her head, she saw two advantages to his suggestion. No cooking, and moments alone to think. She smiled slowly. "Fried chicken isn't considered fast food, is it?"

Luke thought she looked adorable with that hopeful look on her face. "Nope, it's not really fast food."

She let the refrigerator door swing shut. "It's a wonderful idea."

"You won't have any pangs of 'I'm neglecting them because I'm not giving them all their food groups,' will you?"

She grasped at his tease to keep everything light between them. "Buy coleslaw, and I'll be content."

He soaked up the moment as her lips sprang into a quick smile. "I'll go one better."

A chance to relax was too tempting. Val sank onto a chair, stretching her legs to rest her feet on an adjacent chair. "I doubt it. You're doing the cooking and the dishes. I'm blissful."

In passing, he brushed a knuckle across her cheek. "I'll take the girls with me to the store and get them out of your hair. You relax for a while. We'll give you at least an hour."

Excited as usual about going anywhere, with Luke's announcement the twins scampered into the kitchen to Val. Brooke smacked a kiss on Val's cheek. Swinging her doll, Traci hopped the last foot to her and gave her a hug.

While envisioning a leisurely bath, Val strolled with Luke to the door. "I forgot to ask." Without conscious thought, she closed her hand over his forearm below the rolled-up sleeve. "Do you have a badge?"

He studied her eyes for a long moment as if trying to see inside her, trying to see what she seemed intent on avoiding since they'd arrived home. "A badge?"

"Watch them," Val warned. "They have sticky fingers in the store." He thought she was kidding, she realized, hearing his chuckle as he stepped out the door.

He'd learn differently soon.

From a window, Val watched them leave. For the twins' sake, it was important that she and Luke get along well, make them feel secure and loved.

Oh, stop, she berated herself. *Quit playing games with yourself.*

Repeatedly she'd postponed appointments with Harry or any lawyer to discuss divorce. Deep in her heart, she'd hoped everything might change between her and Luke. When she'd married him, she'd assumed they'd be together forever. After watching her mother marry and divorce on a whim, she didn't believe in broken vows. Long ago, she'd decided that promises made were meant to be kept. And weren't the biggest of them all the ones exchanged during a wedding ceremony?

Luke honestly thought he could handle two toddlers. With them in the stroller, he seemed to have everything under control. He learned differently. For only a minute, he looked back at his car to check if he locked the door. In that time, Traci had climbed out of the stroller, waddled away and was bending to pick up a wad of gum stuck to the cement.

Luke snagged her just in time. "Yucky," he said, using her favorite word for anything she didn't like. He turned just in time to see Brooke clambering from the stroller. Luke halted her and tucked her behind her sister.

He gave himself a mental pat on the back and pushed the stroller into the grocery store.

Val had them pegged accurately. In the checkout line, he discovered a candy bar down the front of Brooke's blouse, a box of cookies that Traci was sitting on and a woman's magazine known for explicit advice to single women buried under the cartons of deli coleslaw and potato salad. He set the candy bar on the counter and smoothed the cover of the magazine before returning it to the rack.

The bath had been heavenly. Val had treated herself by taking a glass of ice tea and a paperback in with her. Closing her eyes, she'd sunk into the warm water and relived the tender look in Luke's eyes when they'd stood in the elevator. During those few seconds, pain, tears, even the lost dream seemed no longer clear in her mind. She would like to forget all of that, she realized. If only she wasn't afraid to believe in them again.

Good to his word, Luke didn't return for almost two hours. Dressed in clean shorts and a striped top, Val helped him unpack the grocery bag. "How did it go?"

"No problem." He cast a quick glance at her. By her grin, he gathered she didn't believe him.

"No problem?"

"None."

Val's smile widened as she held up the bag of cookies smashed to crumbs.

"They are fast," he admitted.

Laughing softly, Val whirled away, carrying paper plates and napkins to Traci who stood with arms outstretched. "Here." She set the plates in her arms. "Would you carry these, plea—"

"Lu-cas!"

Brooke's yell pierced through him. He dropped a chicken leg back into the box and darted for the living room. "What?" he asked, calmer now that he saw no disaster or blood.

"Put away." Brooke jabbed a finger at his sneakers blocking the path of her doll's stroller around the coffee table. "Soppy, soppy, soppy," she reprimanded, clucking like an old woman and shaking her head as she picked up one of his shoes.

With the little taskmaster watching him, Luke tossed his shoes in the den. When he returned to the kitchen, Val was holding the phone.

"Oh, of course. We'll be glad to see you." The brightness in her voice sounded forced to him. "Yes, goodbye." She set the receiver back in its cradle and tore past him. "We have to set the table, and get the girls cleaned up," she insisted while capping deli cartons. "Do you think we should dirty pots?" She didn't wait for his answer and began to yank a few out of the cabinet. They clanged as she set them on burners. "She'll think I cooked," she murmured more to herself than him.

Shaking her head, she shoved the pots back into the cupboard. "No that would be dishonest. But what will she think that I didn't cook?'' She smashed the white grocery store bag. ''I should have cooked.'' Coming up for air, she finally made eye contact with him. ''Do something.''

''Slow down a minute.'' Luke blocked her path to the doorway and grabbed both her hands. ''What's going on?''

''Luke, she's coming now. That woman is coming. It's inspection time.''

Chapter Seven

Luke asked only one question. "What do you want me to do?"

Setting the table at top speed, Val spieled a list of orders with the proficiency of an army drill sergeant.

With a promise he'd read two extra stories to the girls at bedtime, Luke persuaded them to pick up their toys in the living room.

While physician's hands disinfected the bathroom sink and swished a toilet bowl brush around in the water, downstairs the vacuum hummed.

Luke thought the girls needed only their hands washed, then spotted what he guessed was that god-awful tasting purple punch on the front of Brooke's blouse. He wiped grubby fingers and sticky faces. "Sit still," he appealed to Brooke while he tugged on a clean sock.

She flopped to her back, twisted to the right, then the left, looking for an escape.

To his amazement, Luke won the battle. "Where are your shoes, Traci?"

Busy tugging at the sock he'd put on her minutes ago, she answered distractedly, "In the washing 'chine."

He'd retrieve them later. Satisfied the girls were clean, he watched the two of them, looking angelic, trod off. But where were they going? he wondered. Indecisively, he stood in the hallway, torn between changing his shirt or playing bloodhound.

"What are you doing?" Val asked on her way up the steps. She definitely sounded a touch panicky to him. With a look he could only interpret as disbelief, she nodded in the direction of his shirt before breezing past him. "Your shirt is wet."

After what he'd just been through, he didn't need any critique of his dress. "And your knees are dirty," he quipped.

She froze in midstride. Glancing down, she groaned at the dark smudges that marked her knees from wiping the kitchen floor of Brooke's spilled punch. "Damn," she muttered low and raced into the bathroom.

"Don't mess up in there," Luke yelled. How often had he heard her say those same words to him before company arrived? On a laugh at the role reversal, he went into the bedroom for a clean shirt.

Wearing only a teddy, she was rummaging in her closet for a dress. "This one?" she asked, whirling toward him and holding up a long white dress with small blue flowers.

Personally he thought she looked great in the teddy. A male preference. He doubted she'd view his opinion as humorous under the circumstances.

"Do you like this one?" she repeated.

He had no chance to answer. Behind him, the phone rang. "Edwin," Luke said a second later, holding the receiver out to her.

She shimmied into her dress first. "Hi, Gramps," she said, turning her back to Luke.

Enormous control kept him from bending forward to kiss her bare back while he tugged up the zipper on the dress. Romantic notions were dispelled as quickly as they formed. Now was not the time.

Downstairs, Luke headed for the garage for Traci's shoes. He was there only a moment. Empty-handed, he returned to the living room to see the twins still clean, sitting quietly over their puzzles. "Traci, where did you say your shoes were?"

"In the washing 'chine."

"They're not there."

Her eyes remained fixed on the puzzle. "Yep."

"No, they're...." Luke stopped himself, sensing the futility of arguing the point with a two year old.

"We can search after dinner," Val suggested on her way to the kitchen.

Dinner in the kitchen wasn't exactly what Luke had planned. Rushed, it lacked the fun and relaxation he'd envisioned when he made the suggestion.

"The woman said she'd be right over," Val grumbled, already rinsing some of the dinner dishes though Traci was still poking at her meal. "So where is she?"

Luke shrugged, and sensing her anxiousness intensifying, he decided retreat was in his best interest. He carried the last of the dishes to the sink and steered the girls into the living room.

On the sofa beside him, Traci wiggled stockinged feet. Sometime before the state worker popped in, he needed to find her shoes.

"Were you looking for these?" Val asked, standing in the arched doorway, dangling Traci's shoes from her fingers.

He was not losing it, he told himself. The sneakers weren't in the washing machine. "Where did you find them? I looked in the..."

"Dishwasher." Looking ready to burst into laughter, Val dropped the shoes beside Traci, then started up the steps.

Dumbfounded, Luke stared down at Traci. "In the..."

Slipping on a shoe, she tore her gaze from the television screen. "Washing 'chine."

Except for a grumble, he said nothing. He crouched to tie her shoes. There was no arguing with a female when she thought she was right. No matter what age she was.

Head bent, he tied one sneaker, then slid the second one on her foot. The sound of paper crinkling behind him made him look up.

Standing at the cupboard, Brooke cradled a box of crackers in one arm and a handful of them in her other hand.

"Hey, put those back."

She gave Luke her best grin, then took off, smashing the crackers as she raced past him in the living room.

On a low groan, he visually followed the trail of cracker crumbs she'd left in her wake.

Calmer with the dishes done, and everything ready, Val finished brushing her hair. She was halfway down the steps when she heard the vacuum. "A problem?" she yelled over the noise, though she'd already spotted the crumbs scattered across the carpet.

Some male thing prevented him from admitting that two pint-size scamps were running him around in circles. He killed the power on the vacuum cleaner. "Nope." By her grin, he knew she didn't believe him. "What did Edwin want earlier?" he asked as he set the vacuum in the nearby closet.

Val glanced at the twins, content now as they listened to the singing of a cartoon lion. "Gramps is going on a date."

Luke shut the closet door. "Who?"

From a distance, thunder rumbled. "Myrna Traynor."

Remembering how devoted she'd seemed to be to her grandmother, he couldn't help asking, "Is that all right with you?"

The idea of her grandfather having someone he enjoyed being with again did please her. "Yes, he—" Val jumped in response to the doorbell. "Calm down," she mumbled to herself, scanning the room. She couldn't afford to be nervous. "Does everything look all right? Do I?"

To soothe, Luke caught her hand. "You look beautiful."

"I like the playroom for the twins," the state worker said. A tall, thin woman in her early fifties, she'd revealed a warm personality more than once during the past hour.

Val had visualized the dour-looking woman being picky and difficult to please. First impressions sometimes were definitely wrong.

Ending her brief play with the girls, the woman handed Brooke a block. "I can see you went through a lot of effort to offer Brooke and Traci comfortable surroundings."

What's your impression of us? Luke wanted to ask. He remained silent as Val ushered the woman to the door.

"This isn't my usual type of case. However, because of the stipulation in the Dawsons' will, you must meet certain criteria for the courts to approve your custodial obligations."

Val bristled. They loved the girls. Why didn't anyone recognize that? "We don't view the girls as an obligation," she cut in before the woman went on.

Surprise widened the woman's eyes. "I'm glad to hear that."

Val squelched a grimace. She shouldn't have flared at the woman. Did she think she was too short-tempered? "We're glad you came," she said, hoping the woman remembered her parting smile and not that outburst.

"Thank you." As Val opened the door, a gust of wind sprayed rain into the room. The woman sighed and placed her hand on her umbrella in preparation of shooting it open once she stepped outside. "You'll be notified about my report."

Val prayed that the disagreeable weather didn't have an affect on the woman's mood. Closing the door, she pivoted toward Luke and the girls who were glued to the Disney movie again. "Luke, I shouldn't have..."

Beside Traci on the sofa, Luke nestled the child closer in the crook of his arm. "All it showed is that you care."

Val chose the closest chair to relax on. "I hope you're right."

"Rain," Brooke murmured with an anxious look at the window. A flash of lightning bolted her from the carpet and onto the chair with Val.

Thunder rumbled, long and loudly.

Burying her face in Luke's chest, Traci clamped her hands over her ears and squeezed her eyes tight.

"Bedtime," Val announced even though fifteen minutes still remained for them to be up. With the storm raging, she thought the sooner they fell asleep, the better.

During their baths, the twins splashed merrily, seeming to completely forget about the weather.

While Val wiped out the tub, Luke read a Christmas story. Brooke's choice. In a voice two octaves lower than normal, he said Santa Claus's lines.

Val entered the room in time to hear his soprano version of Mrs. Claus hurrying her husband out the door to deliver presents. Eyes round, the girls hung on his every word.

Unlike other nights, tonight when he finished the story, neither twin was sleeping. With a tiny hand clutching the rail of her crib, Brooke darted a look toward the window. Another crack of lightning cast the room in an eerie glow.

"Potty," Traci insisted, sounding almost panicky.

Val gathered that her need for cuddling more than a bathroom prompted the demand. Before they returned to the bedroom, she did her best to allay Traci's fear with a story about angels bowling. Calming her didn't mean her mirror image was, too.

"Pee, pee, too," Brooke yelled, waving her arms when Val entered the room.

Though certain her demand was bogus, Val ushered Brooke into the bathroom. Five minutes later, she carried her through the dark hallway to the bedroom.

With a long rumble of thunder, she death-gripped Val's neck. "Tirsty."

Two glasses of water later, both girls were again in bed.

All it took was a glance at Traci to know another request was coming. Her eyebrows knitting with a frown, she relinquished her hold on her blanket and wagged her head. "No Polly."

"It's going to be a long night," Val murmured before retrieving the doll.

With it clutched in her arm, Traci sat in a corner of her crib. Hanging on to the railing with one hand, Brooke gripped her teddy bear. Neither of them looked the least bit tired.

Val elbowed Luke toward the door, and made ready for an escape. The moment she flicked off the light switch, the demands began again.

"Potty," Traci yelled.

"More tirsty," Brooke wailed.

Reaching for the light switch, Val was determined to be firm. "No more drinks of water," she said, gently urging Brooke down and covering her with a blanket. She directed her attention to Traci then. "And no more potty tonight." Only a fool thinks she has control of the situation when dealing with two-year-olds.

With a clap of thunder over the house, the girls screamed as if every monster in the world had appeared before them.

Luke shrugged and crossed to Brooke to soothe her. Quieting Traci, Val nearly winced herself as thunder boomed again above the roof.

At some moment, Luke gave in to his own tiredness and sacked out on the floor, using Brooke's teddy bear for a pillow. Sitting in the rocker, Val closed her eyes. She couldn't deny she was just as sleepy.

It was sometime after midnight when the storm weakened. Sprawled on the floor, Luke looked so peaceful and relaxed, Val hesitated to wake him. She didn't have to. As she moved the rocker forward and pushed to a stand, his head turned in her direction.

"They're sleeping," she whispered, and backed out of the room. Inside the bathroom, Val undressed and slipped on a nightgown. It had been a long day and a confusing one. She couldn't fool herself. Moments with Luke had fostered memories and emotion.

When she opened the door, a narrow path of light flared from the bathroom into the room. She caught movement and saw his silhouette. Stripped of his shirt, his head was bent. "They're a handful," she said on a soft, amused laugh. "But..."

Luke's hands stilled on the snap of his Levi's. "But what?" he asked, unable to look away from the creamy flesh above the lace of whispery-looking cloth.

"There was a time when I thought I'd never be this happy again," she admitted. Lured by the sound of the pounding rain, she ambled to the window. It had stormed the first night they'd made love. Rain had pelted the ground then, too, muffling her moans while his touch had swept a pleasure over her. That night she'd learned the texture of his skin beneath her hands. She'd welcomed him with her body and her heart. "Why couldn't we talk to each other then?"

He knew she meant when they lost Kelly. The need to slip his arms around her closed in on him, but he kept his hands to himself.

Her back to him, she stood ramrod straight, her shoulders back. She'd looked that way at the funeral. Head up, chin out, eyes dry. For months she'd revealed no real emotion, being polite to him as if they'd never exchanged wedding bands, never been lovers, and he hadn't known how to reach her. How could he explain now? When he'd finally let feelings seep into him, he'd already lost her. That was his fault, but how could he have helped her when he'd barely kept a grasp upon sanity himself?

As she turned, the light fell across her eyes—eyes filled with emotion. "I'm sorry," he whispered. "I'm really sorry." The words didn't seem like enough. Raking a hand through his hair, he stepped away. "I'll lock the doors."

Val dragged in air. All that was and could be controlled her. "Luke?" As she called out to him, she'd never been more aware of her vulnerability, nor of his.

She wasn't certain she'd made a decision before this. And whether it was a mistake or not didn't seem to matter. His eyes, like slits in the dimly lit room, never left hers. "I needed you, then." She felt herself taking the last step, reaching out for an old dream. She dropped one strap of her nightgown, and then the other. As if enticing her with the promise of his hands, the cloth slithered over her hips. "And now," she murmured.

Darkness mantled the room, and rain beat in a steady rhythm against the roof. He sucked in a breath, doubting he could take another. For a long moment, he absorbed the subtle sweet scent of a flowery perfume that had been one of the gifts he'd bought her for her last birthday. He closed the distance to her but didn't touch. His blood warming, with something close to reverence, he let his gaze travel over her shadowed body and up to her face. Even beneath the shield of night, he saw a flicker of uncertainty in her eyes, but it left as swiftly as it came.

As her soft breasts pushed into his chest, fantasy blended with reality for him. He felt the heat of her hands on his waist, tugging at his pants, pushing them down, before she swayed the length of her into him. He wanted to say something. He couldn't. Burying his face in her neck, he crushed her to him.

Like the storm outside, one brewed within him. On a groan of pure pleasure, he glided his hands over all that had once been so familiar to him. His mouth raced over her face, tasting. He knew that if she stopped him now, he'd crumble. With his lips on hers, he braced an arm against her back and lowered them to the bed.

All that she'd nearly forgotten was with her again. Val listened to the rain, wondering if he remembered other nights when they'd held each other like this with the sound of raindrops pattering against the windows.

Deepening the kiss, his lips slanted and twisted over hers. Longing slithered through her, and she trembled beneath the hand on her, cupping her breast and caressing her hip. With Luke's gentleness, she recalled wonderful days and nights during the best years of her life. She turned her face, letting her lips play over his jaw, his cheekbone. Need and wants came together as one for her.

As he took his fill of her, lingering, persuading, moving over her as if memorizing, she ached for more. Sensations so alive, so vivid, so familiar, bombarded her. In answer, she skimmed fingers along the hard muscle of his thigh. The magic of every other night they'd had together echoed in the quickening of their breath. A wanting she'd ignored for too long returned, fueled by kisses and caresses.

Her mouth fastening onto his, she felt her heart pounding while his hands taunted and pleasured. Shadows fell across him when he knelt at the foot of the bed. His dark head bent, he curled his fingers around her ankles, and with a slowness meant to drive her mad, his lips and tongue coursed a slow trail up her legs.

She was all hunger and heat suddenly. Gripping his shoulders, she closed her eyes. She didn't need to see. His mouth seared her thigh, her belly, the warmth already waiting for him. The moist path of his tongue whirled her into another world. Wild and dark. And a newness engulfed. What was familiar was rediscovered. He left her breathless, aching, stirring with a demand of her own.

First one shudder, then another passed. A fire burning for him, she shifted, rolling with him on the bed, her legs tangling with his. She heard the soft intimate tone of his voice while she pressed her mouth against his chest, and in lazy circles, she tasted damp flesh.

As she snatched the breath from him, he gave her no time to catch her own. Rain pounded against the window, distant thunder echoed. None of that mattered. They raced against their own storm, one that was urgent and relentless. As if desperate, he dragged her up, and his mouth captured hers. She drew in his tongue, feeling drugged by his taste. The time they'd been apart no longer existed. When he entered her, she knew her memories would include now—this moment, when they came together again.

Lightning flashed, and she saw in his face, in the eyes staring down at her, the same love she'd seen the first time.

Not the soft drizzle outside but the heat of her body curled into his awakened Luke. Beneath the cloak of a gray darkness, he lay still a moment longer. Did he dare believe that all they'd had, all he'd ever wanted, was within his grasp? Was it possible they could start over? He didn't know, but something he'd thought impossible had happened—new hope for them.

Beside him, he felt Val stir. "Stay," he murmured, pulling the blanket up around them. Holding her to him, he shifted and rolled onto his back. He needed her. He needed her smile, her laughter, the gentle understanding in her touch. Tenderly he ran his fingers up and then down her arm to meet her hand. He had missed her, he realized. His loss had gone beyond intimacy. During the past months he'd lost more than his wife. He'd lost his best friend.

With her head on his shoulder, Val opened her eyes. She knew this was the real risk in intimacy. It was more than bodies touching. Hearts mingled even after the warmth of flesh no longer existed. And she was willingly taking this chance, waiting, hoping, that at some moment he'd truly let her back in.

Bending his head, he grazed her temple with his lips. "You're quiet." He searched for some tell-tale sign that she had regrets. The eyes turned up to him smiled.

"I was thinking about last night." With a touch so light she barely felt it, he brushed his mouth across hers. Then once more, as if testing. "That seemed inevitable," she whispered, tracing her finger down the line of hair at his belly.

"Inevitable," he murmured. There was no certainty, he reminded himself, but for the moment, she was his again.

Lazily stretching, Val tasted the flesh at his throat. "They'll be waking up soon."

With her warmth and her scent so near, he didn't want to move, didn't want the moment to end. The burning for her had eased, but the longing for all they'd once had haunted him. He wanted to bury himself in her, never let her go. "Not too soon," he whispered.

"No, not too soon," she answered distractedly, fluttering her fingers along his ribs and over his stomach.

All he could do was groan as her hand moved down.

Chapter Eight

Not bothering with her sneakers, Val strolled downstairs to the kitchen and started the coffee brewer. Because the twins weren't bellowing their favorite song from their cribs, she took the time to sip some coffee before setting the table for breakfast. A hint of sunshine peeked out from behind clouds, casting a sheen on the damp grass. When she left Luke, he'd been burying his face in the pillow, trying to grab a few more minutes of sleep.

She knew it was foolish to wish for too much just because of one night, but they'd been so close again. What if they *could* find their way back to each other?

Climbing the stairs, Val reached the top one and heard the soft huskiness of Luke's voice. Since he wasn't prone to talking to himself, she guessed one or both of the twins had accomplished a new feat this morning—climbing out of the crib.

Val paused at the bedroom doorway.

Traci was snuggling close to him on top of the blanket. "Dog," she announced, pointing to a drawing in the picture book for her audience of two, Luke and her doll Polly.

"What's that?" he asked while smoothing down strands of her hair.

"Car."

Grinning, Luke bent his head closer to her. "And that?"

Her brows pinched with concentration. "Ball."

"No, that's a balloon." He smiled as she tipped her head back to look up at him. "Like you had at your birthday party. Remember them?"

Her gaze returning to the book, she nodded. "Bemember."

As Luke kissed the top of her head, Val said the obvious, "I see we have company." She looked down, feeling a nudge at her hip.

Dragging her teddy bear, Brooke dashed to the bed. At the foot of it, she abandoned the stuffed animal and climbed up. "Lu-cas, up." She gave a hard yank at the sheet and comforter.

Only quick reflexes saved him. Naked, he maintained a firm grip on the covers.

"Get up. Get up," Traci echoed now, bouncing on the bed.

Definitely he had a problem. His mouth twisting in a grin, he shot a look at Val. "Come here." He waited until she'd moseyed closer, then snagged the back of her neck and pulled her face to his.

"Is something wrong?" By the tease dancing in her eyes, she knew exactly what his problem was.

"I can't get up," he whispered in her ear. "If you remember last night, I'm not dressed for company."

A giggle bubbled in her throat. "If I remember right, you're not dressed at all." Pulling back from him, Val couldn't help enjoying his dilemma, but she lifted first Brooke and then Traci down. "Time to get dressed," she announced. Before their protests started, she placed a hand at their backs and steered them toward the door.

Brooke balked and planted her feet. "Lu-cas, up, too," she said impatiently.

For good measure, Luke tightened his grip on the sheet. "I will," he assured her.

On a deep breath of exasperation, Brooke obeyed Val's gentle prodding out the door.

Certain his private time was limited, Luke threw back the covers and rose. Some sixth sense made him snatch up a pillow and ram it against his groin.

Standing in the doorway, Val gave him a lengthy look, her lips twitching as she battled a grin. "I've seen it all. Hurry." Her laughter broke through the moment she stepped away.

With a good twenty minutes to spare while Val dressed the girls and got breakfast ready, Luke headed out for his morning run. Funny but everything looked different this morning. The grass a little greener, the sun a little brighter. Romantic thinking, maybe. But he felt too good to question such thoughts beyond that.

He waved to Travis Donovan as he and his son drove by. The five-year-old jabbered nonstop whenever he came into Luke's office. Would the twins be like that at the same age?

On Lexington, Luke slowed his pace to cool down. Would the girls be eager on their first day of school? He thought Traci would. She seemed to thrive on new adventures. Brooke, though, tended to analyze everything first, but she did like books and her toy computer.

He gave his head a shake. *Slow down.* One night with Val didn't mean she was willing to try forever again.

Winded from his morning run, he drew several long breaths before he entered the house.

Together, the twins were chanting Val's name and banging on what Luke assumed was the bathroom door.

Val answered them, but whatever she'd said didn't prevent the clash of wills.

"No—no," Traci yelled.

"Don't," Brooke returned an octave louder than her sister. As Luke hit the top stair and came into view, Brooke wailed. "Lu-cas." Scrambling to a stand, she screamed his name again and wobbled toward him on one of Val's high heels.

When Traci clumped toward him on the other shoe, he guessed what the quarrel was about. "You'd better put those back, or you're both going to be in trouble." Looking put-upon, they stomped ahead of him into his bedroom. Val's shoes were strewn everywhere. "We've got work to do." Somehow he ignored the two guileless grins raised to him. "Fast," he said, and bent to get the girls started.

Val found the three of them kneeling outside her wall-to-wall closet and stacking shoe boxes. Smiling, she went to the kitchen to start breakfast.

An hour later, Val took the girls into the backyard with a warning to stay away from Luke and the lawn mower. She tipped back the brim of the baseball cap she wore for gardening and squinted up when Luke stopped beside her and leaned on the handle of the lawn mower. "I can't believe she ate three pancakes," Val said in amazement about Brooke.

It took a moment for him to answer. Her face glowed with a fine sheen of perspiration, her eyes looked bright with humor, her hair tousled from the baseball cap she'd just removed. He'd seen her look the same way during a far more intimate and private moment. "She was hungry." He came up behind her and whispered in her ear, "So am I." As she leaned back against him, he had to make himself remember they weren't alone.

Over her shoulder, she turned a sympathetic look up at him. "Poor Lucas."

Though she didn't know why she was saying the words, from nearby, sitting in her sandbox, Brooke echoed, "Poor Lu-cas."

"How did I ever live without all this female compassion?" he asked.

Val turned in his arms and kissed him quickly. "Face it," she said with a smile. "You're the only male in this house. You'll be treated like a king."

"Or ganged up on," he returned, caressing her hip before he stepped away to finish mowing the front lawn.

Contentment sweeping over her, Val dug more weeds from the garden.

"Dis a weed?" Traci asked from her kneeling position beside Val.

Val gave the zinnia in her hand a wistful look. "No, sweetheart, that's a flower."

Traci shrugged and eyed her sister merrily dumping sand from one plastic bucket to another. Minutes later, as Val expected, Traci took off to join her.

Adjusting her cap against the glare of the sun, Val saw Luke strolling back. His face beaded with perspiration, he slid down against the trunk of the tree that shaded her garden. "Did you talk to my mom about sitting with the girls tomorrow night?" he asked while brushing knuckles across a sweaty brow.

Val actually was looking forward to Neil and Cindy's party now. "She said she'd be over by six o'clock, so I'd be free to get ready." Taking a breather herself, she plopped down beside him. "The ledgers at the office are a mess, Luke." She decided someone needed to know what she'd discovered during the past few days.

"Blame Neil. He may be a dentist, but he keeps thinking he's Mr. Accountant."

Looking down, Val yanked off her gardening gloves. "I noticed Everett didn't pay you again," she said about an elderly patient of his, a local farmer.

Luke eyed the pile of weeds already pulled. "He promised us a bushel of lemons."

Val slanted an amused look at him. "We'll have to drink lemonade for the rest of our lives to use up all the lemons he gave us last time."

His gaze flicked away from hers to settle on her lips. "I like lemonade."

Unable to resist, Val swayed on her knees toward him and stroked his jaw. "You have a kind heart."

"And you have a beautiful mouth." With a fingertip, he traced the line of it. This time would be forever, he decided. It had to be, or he'd die without her.

"Company?" Val asked, turning her head in response to the sound of a car pulling onto the driveway.

Because they'd anticipated no one, Luke shrugged and listened. When the engine stopped, he pushed to a stand. "I'll see who's here."

Val tossed the weeds into the yard garbage can. She'd expected Luke to return. When he hadn't after a few minutes, she scooted the girls inside to play with their dollhouse, then wandered into the living room with a can of root beer.

Harry Cannon, their lawyer, sat on the chair across from Luke. Gloom and doom were written on Harry's face as he greeted her. "Valerie."

She forced a smile, hoping one of them returned it. Neither of them did. "What? Has something happened?"

"I'm afraid so." Harry hunched forward. "I came over as soon as I learned."

Nerves danced within her. "Learned about what?"

Disturbed since Harry briefly explained the reason for his visit, Luke reached up for her wrist and urged her to sit beside him on the sofa. "Charlene wants guardianship of the girls." Because she visibly paled, he slid an arm around her shoulders. "It might not be as bad as it sounds."

"No, of course not," Harry agreed. "But as Joe's natural cousin, Charlene believes she has that right."

"Wait a minute." Clutching the can tighter in her hand, Val shook her head. "I don't understand. Why? Why does she want them? From what I've heard about Charlene, she never kept it a secret that motherhood wasn't in her plans. And I remember Carrie saying that Charlene hadn't talked to Joe in six years. She doesn't even know the girls. She and George don't have any by choice. At least, that's what everyone believes. Why would she suddenly want Joe's children?"

Over Val's head, Luke saw the twins standing in the kitchen doorway curiously watching them. "Why don't we stop in at your office later, Harry, to discuss this?"

Harry's round face broadened with a deeper frown. "We'll challenge this." He offered Val a strained smile as Luke walked him to the door. "Valerie, don't worry."

Oh, but she was. Obeying the gentle grip of Luke's fingers beneath her elbow, she moved mechanically with him back into the kitchen, halting at the refrigerator. "Luke, this doesn't make sense." Facing him, she gripped his shirt sleeve while she fought to keep a hold on the panic threatening to rise within her.

Luke knew of no way to make this easier for her. All he could do was give her facts. "Joe and Charlene hadn't talked since Joe's dad died." The problems within the Dawson family had been public knowledge back then, but only a native of New Hope, like him, would remember what had provoked the feud. "When she was a kid, Charlene's parents died and she went to live with Joe and his father. She was wild," Luke admitted. "When she was in her last year of high school, she started seeing George Evans."

Charlene's love life didn't interest Val. What she wanted was for him to assure her that Charlene couldn't get the twins. Determined to stay calm, Val asked in a firm voice, "The man she's married to?"

Luke maintained a fixed expression. He wished for earlier moments when happiness had brightened her eyes. "Only he was married before, then—when she started seeing him."

"You mean she was having an affair with a married man?"

"For someone like Joe's dad, a pillar of the church, her behavior had been unforgivable. Joe's dad was furious. He demanded she stay away from George. She was always headstrong. When she refused, Joe's dad stopped talking to her."

Val wondered why he felt compelled to tell her so much about the past when all she cared about was what was going to happen next. "But Charlene did eventually marry George."

"After a messy divorce, he married Charlene. Though everything rightfully would have been passed down to Joe, Joe's father had taken care of Charlene since she was ten and had always treated her as if she were his own daughter. When he died six years ago, she learned he'd left everything, including the family business, to Joe. Enraged, Charlene insisted that some of the property and a portion of the business belonged to her. Joe refused. She even went to court and fought Joe for it, and she lost. By then, she already wasn't speaking to Joe."

Val felt a dull throbbing at her temples. "Then why would she want Joe's children?" Her voice trailed off. She knew the answer. This wasn't about the twins. "The girls' wealth. As Joe's children, the twins are the heirs to everything?"

"Might be a good incentive for Charlene to want them." Luke curled a hand over her shoulder. Beneath his fingers, he felt a tenseness that contradicted her calm expression. He didn't bother to mouth words that she shouldn't worry. He knew better now. He'd done that before when they'd waited silently together, counting the seconds ticking by as their tiny daughter fought for her life. "We'll see Harry—" He stopped as a blood-curdling scream rang in the air.

On his heels, Val dashed from the kitchen to see Brooke plopped on the floor in the foyer, tears running down her cheeks while she hugged her knee. Seeing no blood, Val felt her heart slow a couple of beats. Even before she dropped beside Brooke, she'd quickly surmised the injury as nothing more than a scrape. The moment she cuddled Brooke in her arms, her wailing stopped.

"Ow-ee," she insisted on a sniff.

Luke brushed a thumb across her cheek to dry a tear. "We'd better get a bandage for that. A glow-in-the-dark one," he suggested.

On another sniff, she nodded her head, obviously satisfied with his remedy.

Val left him doctoring and wandered back to the kitchen. Hazy sunlight streamed through the lacy curtain. She wanted to believe Charlene had no rights, but she had read about too many custody battles between biological and adoptive parents. She and Luke weren't the adoptive parents, only guardians, and Charlene hadn't given birth to the twins. But to the court, if Charlene was serious, Val knew she and Luke would be in a battle between strangers and a blood relative. Strangers, by court standards, seemed the losers lately.

Val pulled the sink plug and listened to water gurgling down the drain. None of it made sense to her. Who loved them, who'd be best for them, was all that should have mattered. The twins deserved to be raised by parents who cared about their scraped knees, who share their disappointments and happiness. Who didn't care if there was one dollar or a hundred thousand dollars in a trust fund for them.

"I bet you have things to do," Luke said unexpectedly from behind her. "I have a few appointments this afternoon but I'm free until we see Harry later. What if I play Mr. Mom?"

He was worried about her, Val realized. Nerves frayed, she was grateful for his suggestion. It might help if she concentrated on the overload of work she'd brought home from the office. "How can I refuse such an offer?"

Her smile didn't reach her eyes, but Luke said nothing. Peace of mind wasn't something another person could supply.

For the next hour he spent time with the girls at the park. They raced from the swings to the teeter-totter to the slide, back to the teeter-totter, then the swings. He gave Val credit. Watching them was a full-time job.

Because of the appointment with Harry, Luke planned to feed the girls an early lunch. The moment they entered the kitchen, Traci plopped on the floor to bang on pots. More interested in food, Brooke stayed close. Luke pulled a stool over to the counter and set her beside him. As he spread peanut butter on bread, she swiped a finger at it. "Want jelly on this?"

"No," she mumbled while licking her finger.

He couldn't resist a tease. "What about on this?" he asked, grabbing the sticky finger.

"No!"

"Okay. One stick-to-the-roof-of-your-mouth sandwich coming up."

"No!"

Ignoring what he'd learned was her favorite word, Luke cut the sandwich into quarters.

"No!" she bellowed as he lifted her down from the stool.

"Lunch isn't going to be peaceful," Luke mumbled to the air. Not to be bested by a two year old, he crouched and whispered into Brooke's ear.

Docilely she let him sit her in her high chair and began eating her sandwich. In the other high chair, Traci greeted his lunch with total disgust, placing a hand to her head and pursing her lips until he handed her a banana. Luke decided whatever order she ate everything was fine with him, just so long as she ate.

Having played audience to the scene, Val would have been impressed with his parental persuasion if she hadn't thought he'd done something sneaky. "Do you have a secret?" she asked.

"A little one. I've promised to be the guest at a tea party," he said, watching her smile grow with his explanation.

Through lunch, the twins babbled in a language meant for interpretation only by other two-year-olds.

As Traci stuck a finger in her mouth and scraped at the sandwich clinging to the roof of it, Val poured her a glass of milk. ''Why didn't you put jelly on the sandwiches?''

The edge of amusement in her voice relaxed him. She's dealing with this mess, Luke believed. He saw no reason why they should have to worry. They were back together, who could prove anything had ever been wrong? ''They didn't want it,'' he answered.

She thought he needed some advice to survive fatherhood. ''They don't want a lot of things. Just put it on next time,'' she said low in his ear before lifting an impatient Brooke from her high chair.

What did he know? He was still new at this.

Chapter Nine

On the way to Harry's office, Luke and Val dropped the girls off at the library.

Waiting for them, Val's grandfather took each twin's hand. "Don't worry," he said to Val before he led the girls to the library's storytelling area set up for preschoolers.

The moment Val stepped outside again, she gave up on the smile she'd plastered on her face for her grandfather.

Luke offered what sounded like a lame assurance to his own ears. "Harry will help us." Reaching for her hand, he was surprised at how icy it felt.

With effort, Val worked up a weak smile because she knew he wanted to see it. "I know he will. I'm all right."

Luke wondered if that was true. She was a nurturing person, one who spent hours with the flowers in her garden, freeing them of weeds. She'd always wanted children. Even before they were married, she'd told him that she thought being a mother was the most special job in the world. She'd already lost once. He wasn't certain how she'd handle losing again.

When Luke followed her into the office at twelve-thirty, she was already engaged in conversation with the receptionist, an ex-girlfriend of Luke's and now the mother of three. She beamed at them as she asked about the twins.

Val heard herself answering but couldn't recall what she said. Nerves on edge, she laced her fingers together. At the opening of Harry's office door, she jerked forward in her haste.

In the doorway, he placed a fatherly hand on her shoulder. "You look like you could use some coffee."

"No, I really don't want any." Val crossed the plush beige carpeting to reach one of the leather chairs in front of his desk.

"Lucas?"

Luke didn't miss Harry's sympathetic expression. No amount of compassion would help, Luke wanted to say. Just help us keep those girls. "Me, either, Harry. Thanks." Because he felt an urge to pace, when he'd settled on a chair, he deliberately stretched out his legs.

Rounding his desk, Harry snatched up a manila folder. "Obviously you both want me to get to the matter at hand," he said, sitting.

Val did her best to respond to his smile. "We're concerned, Harry," she said with a quietness that amazed her.

"That's understandable. Before all you had to do was satisfy the court. Joe Dawson's cousin causes some complications if she challenges your guardianship."

"So how do we challenge back?" Luke pressed his point. "All of this is because he got the family business and she got nothing. Can we emphasize that to the judge?"

"We could try to prove what you're saying, but frankly, I believe it would be impossible."

"Everything belongs to them, no one else," Luke said heatedly.

"Easy, Lucas," Harry soothed, making Luke aware of how riled he sounded. "We have a lot in our favor. You and Valerie are well thought of in the community. Financially you're in an excellent position to raise the twins, and have not seemed interested in their inheritance."

"We aren't," Val insisted. "We don't even care about any of that."

Harry softened his voice. "I know."

Val forced herself to relax and lean back in the chair. She needed to stay calm through all of this.

"Also," Harry went on, "the court would look favorably on the fact that Lucas is a doctor. And your marriage is stable." He smiled. "In fact, it's considered one of the best in town. That's the most important factor because Joe and Carrie specifically insisted on your having a solid marriage."

Val willed herself not to look at Luke. What if others learned that it hadn't been so solid, that they'd considered divorce? Was he wondering the same thing right now?

"However, I have to warn both of you. You're going to be asked some discomforting questions."

Tightly, Val gripped the strap of her shoulder bag. "Such as?" Instead of immediately answering her, Harry pushed away from his desk and stood. Val's stomach clenched. Was he stalling or hesitant? What was so difficult for him to say?

"Harry, what is it?" Luke asked, growing impatient.

When he dragged a chair closer to them, Val sensed their friend, not their lawyer, now sat in front of them. "You may be asked about Kelly."

Luke hadn't expected this. "What kind of questions?"

Harry glanced at Val before answering him. "How she died."

"You know that. She was born with a heart valve defect." Val fought to sound steady. "The doctors said they could operate, but it was risky because Kelly was too young and too weak. And within hours of her birth, she died." It took effort, but Val managed to ask the question nagging her since he'd mentioned Kelly. "Why would they want to know any of that?"

"Valerie, I'm sorry if this is upsetting, but you need to be prepared."

"Please answer me. Why would they ask about Kelly?"

"If Charlene does contest your guardianship, her lawyer is going to look for reasons, not why she should have them, but why you shouldn't. Such as, are the twins a substitute for the daughter you lost?''

Val stifled a moan. "Oh, this is incredible. No. You know that isn't true. You know that Luke and I aren't the kind of people who wouldn't value each child for herself. We even talked about having another child.''

Some of the tension tightening Harry's features softened. "Is that right? That's good." He rose to return to his chair behind the desk. "It means you were ready to go on with your lives, to start a family again.''

Val met Luke's gaze and silently pleaded with him not to mention that she'd refused when he'd suggested having another baby. ''The twins really aren't a substitute for Kelly,'' she said as much to assure him as Harry.

"I believed that to be true, but you have to know the direction of the questions you'll be asked." He suddenly chuckled as if he felt foolish. "No affairs?''

Luke felt a rarely seen temper rising. "Come on, Harry. You know both of us better than that.''

"I had to ask, Lucas. I don't want any surprises in court." Harry closed the manila folder containing his notes. "Okay, if neither of you feel that we'll have some bombshell dropped on us, then I guess we're ready for Charlene and her lawyer. Instead of attacking Charlene, I believe we should point out how right you both are for them. Chances are you should get the twins. It's what their parents wanted. We'll emphasize that. We'll mention your positions in the community, the stability of your marriage, your desire for a family,'' he said, and swiveled his wing-armed chair away from the desk.

Luke took Harry's cue and rose. At Val's movement beside him, he sidled close to her. Placing his hand at the small of her back, he listened to Harry's final words about presenting them as the town's model couple. Beneath his fingers, Luke felt her spine straighten as if she were fighting not to slouch beneath some burden. The same burden, no doubt, that was suddenly weighing him down. What if the court learned they'd been on the verge of divorce? No matter what their relationship was now, that they'd considered divorce meant their marriage wasn't so perfect.

Quietness accompanied their drive to the library. When the twins were in their car seats, Traci chattered away about a book with a horsey while Brooke sucked on her afternoon bottle.

Because Luke had been so silent, Val deliberately forced some inconsequential conversation. "I'll take the car," she said. "I told your mother I'd stop at the hotel and tell her what happened."

"She'll want to know," Luke murmured, trying to snap himself from thoughts that harbored a future of trouble. Glancing at his rearview mirror, he saw Brooke swinging her bottle. "Val, you'd better take that from her before she bops Traci with it."

Only a second passed, no more, before Val looked over her shoulder. Quicker than seemed possible, Brooke tossed the bottle out the window. "Oh." Val felt a laugh bubble up. "Luke, you have to stop."

He swiveled a questioning look at her. "What?"

"Brooke threw her bottle out the window."

"Bad Brooke," her twin announced, wagging her finger at her sister.

"Be quiet," Brooke screeched at an ear-piercing level.

"Brooke, be quiet," Traci yelled equally as loud.

Val hushed both of them while Luke hustled out of the car, mumbling under his breath. Watching him cautiously inch his way down an embankment to retrieve the bottle, she thought about parents gushing over sweet little babies who cooed softly and demanded nothing but a dry diaper and a bottle. She and Luke had caught only glimpses of that stage with the twins when they visited Joe and Carrie. That was the easy time, she decided. What they were doing was a lot tougher. They were raising two children, dealing with their tantrums and stubbornness. She viewed all that as a passing phase. She looked past the little squabbles about possession of toys. Too many other times they revealed a loving and warmth with each other, or for no reason at all, they'd climb on Luke's or her lap for a hug. They were sweet and caring. They were all that she'd longed for.

By the time Luke slid behind the steering wheel, Val had quieted the girls. Still solemn-looking, he handed her the bottle coated with dirt, then twisted around toward Brooke.

"Me sorry." Her bottom lip trembling, she looked like she'd burst into tears if he looked at her the wrong way.

Emotions high already, Val felt a tug that threatened tears as he leaned back toward Brooke.

Her arms flung around his neck, and she smacked a kiss on his cheek, close to his eye. "Love you."

Luke took a moment to wiggle fingers and stir her giggle. He'd failed one child. He wouldn't make the same mistake with another. "And I love you."

"Traci, too," Traci piped in, eager to get in on the game.

"Both of you," he said, stretching to tickle a sensitive spot on her kneecap.

Val felt a catch in her heart. They had to keep the girls. Being a parent had nothing to do with conception. Willingly they weathered good and bad moments with the girls for one reason, the only reason that mattered—they loved them, and Joe and Carrie had believed they were the best ones to raise and care for the girls. Surely the court would see that.

She held on to that thought while driving to the hotel after dropping Lucas at his office. Tucking small, warm hands in her own, she led the girls into the hotel lobby.

The instant they entered, Irene skirted the registration desk to meet them. "Where's my kiss?" she asked brightly and knelt for a hug. Over their heads, she sent Val a concerned look, then stood. "Come with me." She took the twins to a room adjacent to the lobby that seemed to exist for one reason—the big screen television.

While they watched an afternoon cartoon, Val summarized the meeting with Harry.

The line between Irene's brows deepened with her frown. "Well, Charlene won't get much support from anyone around here." As the twins wandered over, Irene spoke softly, "Don't worry. My son has always fought for what he wanted. Even as a boy, whenever he wanted something, no matter how many difficulties were in his way, he'd face them head-on. Lucas never gave up."

No, he didn't, Val reminded herself. He'd been the one who'd insisted Kelly would be all right until all hope had been gone.

"Let me take the twins home with me," Irene said, cutting into Val's thought. "I'll bring them over later."

Val considered a few errands she needed to make. "I haven't seen Faith in a while, and I did want to stop at her shop."

"Then, go."

A few minutes later, dangling a bag from Homer's Shoe Repair, Val ambled over to the Baby Boutique. In the display window with its soft pink lights, Faith had arranged several jumpers and toddler play clothes.

Val strolled to the door and saw the Closed sign. Rarely did Faith close the shop in the middle of the day. Was she ill? And even if she wasn't feeling well, she had a part-time helper. Where was Beth?

Concerned suddenly for her friend, she decided to play sleuth. She drove down Lee Street then made a few right turns to reach the street where Faith lived. Not seeing her friend's car in the driveway, Val drove toward home to make a few phone calls.

Keeping his mind on work hadn't been easy. Luke ushered Sue Ellen toward the door that led to the reception area of his office. "You'd feel better if you got more sleep," he said, offering the diner owner his usual advice.

Her heavily made-up eyes smiled at him. "You always say that."

"And you don't listen."

She sighed exaggeratingly. "I'll try."

Luke pivoted back to his examining room. Since he'd arrived at the office, he'd assured Minny that she didn't have some exotic disease on her big toe and he'd given the Duran's one-year-old son an immunization shot.

Before he left for the day, he whipped X rays from an envelope to check the healing process of an eleven-year-old's broken arm.

The click of the door opening behind him made him look away from the X ray he'd been studying.

Edwin poked in his head. "Luke, could you give me a minute?"

In the past, Luke had done the unthinkable among most doctors, he'd made house calls. Turning down his wife's grandfather at any time was inconceivable. "Sure, come on in."

"What did the lawyer tell you?" Edwin asked before closing the door behind him.

"We have a fight ahead of us."

Edwin nodded his head as if prodding fate. "You'll win."

Luke hoped he was right. "So what's wrong?" he asked. He had checked with the doctor who'd given Edwin his last physical. He was in excellent health for a man of his age who'd had a heart bypass.

"I have a problem."

Luke gestured toward a chair. With so much happening, could Val handle worry about her grandfather's health, too? "Why don't you tell me what's bothering you?"

Edwin didn't sit. "I'm wondering if I can live up to her expectations," he said, shifting his weight from one foot to the other in the manner of an anxious teenager facing his date's father.

It took a second before Luke comprehended what expectations Edwin was talking about. Somehow he managed to remain expressionless. "Her?"

"Myrna," he said as if Luke were a dolt for asking.

"By expectations—you mean, sexually?"

"Of course, I do." Edwin scowled at him. "I'm old, not dead."

Luke stifled a grin. "Has she said she has expectations?"

"She's a young filly. Younger than me. I don't think I could manage much more than once a day."

"Once a day?" Lucas barely restrained his own incredulity. "Edwin, you're seventy-one years old. If you can manage once a day, you don't need any help."

His eyes twinkled with a smile. "Then I'm normal?"

"Better than." Luke touched Edwin's shoulder as they drifted toward the door. "But be responsible."

"Right-o." He gave Luke a quick salute. "Safe sex." Whistling, he shut the door behind him.

Strolling up to the back door of the house, Val breathed in the scent of the late blooming flowers she'd planted the year before. With everything that ends, a newness begins. Sometimes it was so hard to remember that.

She unlocked the door, then flicked on the radio and hummed along with a Whitney Houston love song.

When dinner was started, she dialed Jenny's number. As she waited for Jenny to answer the phone, she opened cans of tomato paste and sauce.

Val poured the red sauce into a pot while she talked with Jenny about her concern with Faith. "I'll try calling her again," she told Jenny.

"Are you going back to the store?"

"Tomorrow probably. No, maybe the next day," she answered, remembering Cindy's party.

"Okay. Maybe I'll see you there," Jenny returned.

Val balanced the receiver between her jaw and shoulder. "On what excuse?"

"No excuse. I need to buy a gift for my cousin's new baby. What are you going for?"

Val told Jenny about the jumpers she'd seen. Through the screen door, she heard the sound of a car engine and stretched the telephone cord to look out the window. "I've got to go. Luke's home."

"I always believed in second chances," Jenny said encouragingly.

"I'm becoming a believer in that, too," Val admitted. With a quick goodbye, she set down the receiver. Except for the mess with Charlene, everything seemed perfect. But was it? she wondered, recalling how quiet Luke had been after the meeting with Harry.

As the door behind her opened and closed, she turned to deliver a smile. "Hi. You're home earlier than I expected." She studied him closely, saw none of the recognizable fatigue in his eyes, but neither could she read his mood.

"I left thinking you might want help with the twins. Where are they?" he asked, aware of no banging or singing or bickering.

"With your mother." Val moved toward him, needing to recapture closeness, and lovingly ran her fingers down the nape of his neck.

One corner of his lips twitched before a slow smile formed. "For how long?"

It seemed like another lifetime since they'd made love during the day. "They're at your mother's and won't be back until later." She closed her eyes as his lips caressed her collarbone. "I missed you today."

"Can you leave this for a while?" he murmured against her lips, indicating the food on the stove.

"You have something else planned?"

With deft fingers, he pulled down the zipper of her dress. "Something."

Tilting her head back, she gave his mouth freedom to explore her throat. "Such subtlety." As she tugged his shirttail from his pants, he gave her no time to take a breath. His lips on hers, he tangled his fingers in her hair. Desire came quickly as if the need had been there for hours. With unsteady fingers, she tugged at the buttons on his shirt. Gliding her hands across his stomach muscles, she felt a desperateness for him pulling at her. When his hand raced over her, she briefly opened her eyes. The stove seemed to stare back at her. "Not here," she said on a quick breath.

"What?" His breath was hot against her bare shoulder.

"Not here," she repeated. "The door isn't locked."

It took effort to slow down. Filled with her taste, he buried his face in her hair for a second before he slid an arm under her knees. The walk to the bedroom would kill him. He was sure of that. "We should have

bought a single level house." Beneath his lips, he felt
her smile while he climbed the stairs.

They practically fell onto the bed. Hurrying each
other, he pulled clothes from her. She yanked them
from him. All she'd brought into his life was with him
again. Tenderness. Excitement. Heat.

With hands as restless as his, Val skimmed the warm
dampness of his flesh. For a little while, she could
forget everything except the waves of sensation he
promised with every touch, with every kiss, with every
gentle stroke of his tongue. He caressed. He beckoned. Wild with need, she melted.

Fire spread through her. She heard him muttering
something while she sought every inch of him and
tasted the saltiness of his skin.

As if torn from his throat, her name slipped from
his lips. Urgent, hungry now, he pinned her beneath
him.

Val opened her eyes and stared into the face of her
husband. Late afternoon sunlight streamed into the
room, slanting shadows across the smooth planes and
rough bristle of his jaw. Her hands ran over him, caressing the taut muscles of his shoulders and back and
buttocks.

On a soft moan, she arched against him, then called
his name. With the honesty of emotion that had
bound them for four years, he slipped into her. Flesh
warmed flesh. Impatience urged them. Together
again, they surrendered to the pulsing needs whirling
them into a mindless world. And she lost herself—in
his eyes filled with the darkness and warmth of passion—in the heat—in the fullness of him.

Breathless, she sighed and strained to draw him deeper. Swift and demanding, waves of sensation lapped over her. She gasped to keep pace. They moved as one, with and against each other, harsh and unsteady breaths dueting, and she clung as she'd wanted to during every moment they'd been apart. Then with a breathy whisper, she floated with him, drifting, letting the stunning pleasure wash over her.

Languidly Val caressed the muscular flesh of Luke's hip before dragging herself from the bed. It had taken effort to leave his side, but choices didn't exist. In jeans and a T-shirt, she hurried from the bathroom. At the bedroom doorway, she gave him one last look to see him tugging on jeans.

Val flew down the steps. The tangy smell of the sauce bubbling in a saucepan permeated the air and drifted to her. She barely rescued it in time. "We almost didn't have dinner," she said with a laugh, plopping lasagna noodles into a pot of boiling water when Luke wandered in. Sighing, she stilled as he came up behind her and gently splayed his fingers over her belly. During those moments upstairs, she understood him. They were one, so much a part of each other that she wondered how they'd ever separated. "This could be dangerous," she murmured in response to him nuzzling her neck.

He wasn't ready to let her go, not now—not ever, he realized in that moment. "Remember the first meal you cooked?" he asked, gliding his tongue across skin that rivaled the softness of velvet.

Sensation clouded her mind. "A towel on the stove caught on fire."

"Yeah, and while we put out the fire, you burned the dinner." With the remembrance, humor flowed over him. "It was a great night."

Val had thought so, too. They'd sat in the bedroom away from the rest of the smoke-filled rooms. "Great meal."

Like then, her scent, her taste, her softness were all he could think about. "Cereal," he answered thickly.

"In bed." Val bit back a sigh as his lips traced a path downward. "We spilled it."

"And made love on the rug." One more time, he kissed the side of her neck.

She angled a lazy-looking grin up at him. "We had fun."

"That we did." Before heat rushed through him again, he let his hands slip off of her, and he pivoted toward the refrigerator.

Warm and content, she understood now what he'd been doing since he'd arrived home. He was striving for normalcy despite the threat that promised to snatch away the happiness they'd found. Val sprinkled basil on top of the cheese, then capped the spice bottle. "How was the rest of your day?"

He thought about Edwin's visit. "Unique. What about yours?" he asked while tucking his shirt into his pants.

With a look over her shoulder, she cracked a smile. "Not as much fun. But interesting."

"I expect that it was," he said while washing his hands to tear at lettuce.

Val stretched for a casserole dish on a top shelf. "They're so different. The twins, I mean. Traci is always moving while Brooke is so quiet—sometimes," she added because the little one was a typical two year old.

Luke paused in slicing a tomato. "Night and day maybe. But if they want something like a cookie, they're of one mind."

Were they, too? Val wondered because they'd been dodging discussion about their visit to Harry's office. She began layering the noodles, sauce and cheese into the casserole dish. "I don't think Charlene's lawyer could learn that we nearly separated, do you?" she asked softly, unable to keep inside any longer what had bothered her ever since they'd left Harry's office.

He'd heard a wistfulness in her voice. She was scared. He knew he was reading the emotion accurately, and wanted to tell her that they'd be all right this time, but a judge with no idea what the twins meant to them would make a decision. And how could he convince her everything would go their way when he wasn't sure himself?

At his silence, Val cast a worried glance at him. He kept staring ahead, his chiseled features so tense they almost looked as if they were carved from stone. "No one knew but Jenny and Gramps, and they wouldn't say anything to anyone," she said.

He still said nothing, making Val more nervous. *Don't go strong and silent on me,* she wanted to yell. "What aren't you saying? Do you feel that you don't want to bother with what we'll have to go through to get them?"

Luke's gaze cut to her. That he'd heightened her worry came through clearly. He swore at himself before answering. "I want them," he assured her. Questions still clouded her eyes. She needed more, an explanation, he realized. It had been so long since he'd shared thoughts with her. "Ever since we left Harry's office, I've thought how a custody battle might affect the twins, especially if it drags out. It doesn't matter about us, but they don't need that."

Val felt the weakened link in their marriage tightening. His desires, his worries, were as important as her own. Was he finally realizing that if they didn't really talk to each other, no amount of passion would bind them? "We'll protect them," she said, feeling more confident since she knew now they were of one mind about the twins.

While she placed the casserole in the oven, Luke concentrated on rinsing the lettuce. Protecting someone else from hurt wasn't easy. Who knew that better than he? Because so much uncertainty shadowed them, he put his arms around Val. He wanted to give her his strength. He needed to feel her softness. "I know what you want," he whispered against her hair. "I'd give it to you if I could. I'd give you anything you wanted."

With a few words, he nearly stirred the tears she'd resisted all day whenever she considered losing the twins. On a deep breath, she vowed she wouldn't fall apart. She'd given in to her sadness once before and had learned it didn't help.

"We'll have them with us," he said even as he carried doubts within. What else could he say? All he could do was be near for her, prove to her what he'd failed at before. When she needed him, he'd be there for her.

"We're home," a voice, definitely his mother's, sang out from the vicinity of the front door.

Tilting back her head, Val looked up at him. She saw the strength in his face that she felt in the arms holding her, and she wished she could give him an assurance that she really wasn't the woman he'd married. She'd gotten stronger. She'd had to. "Don't worry so about me," she whispered.

But he did. He'd lost her before. He didn't want to again.

Chapter Ten

Beneath a hearty wind, a branch of the tree outside the bedroom window tapped against the glass. A gray morning sky threatened a drizzle before noon. With thoughts of reading the morning newspaper before the twins awoke, Luke headed for the bedroom doorway. Even before he reached it, he heard giggling and what distinctively sounded like a chorus of "Whee!"

At the end of the hallway, Val stood outside the twins' bedroom. Short, pale blue shorts snugly gripped her hips and showed off enough leg to make him wish they were still in bed. "Are they awake?" he asked, strolling closer.

"Have a look." She released a low, husky laugh and swept an arm toward the room.

Sitting in her crib, Traci was tossing shredded bits of tissue in the air. From her bed, Brooke gleefully watched the papers flying upward and then descending to the carpet.

"Obviously it snowed in here this morning," Val whispered laughingly.

Luke shifted his hand to the sharp angle of her hip. "I never liked shoveling snow."

Turning, Val placed her hands against his chest. "How did I know you were going to say that?"

"You're a mother."

Her heart swelled with the unexpected words. *She* was a mother now. At one time she'd thought that would never happen.

"Mothers know everything, don't they?" he teased.

Val tipped her chin up. "Everything," she returned, giving him a quick kiss before entering the room to play maid.

Despite his words, he followed her in to help. An idea had been forming before Val had gotten out of bed. Willing to do the cleanup alone, she nudged Luke out the door with her request.

The twins were ready, dressed and fed by the time he returned with helmets and carrier seats for Val's and his bikes.

Impatiently waiting beside Luke, Traci shifted from one foot to the other. "Big bike," she said, her blue eyes sparkling when Luke lifted her to the seat on the back of his bicycle.

"Yep." Over her head, Luke saw pleasure flash in Val's eyes that she'd surprised the twins with their plan for a bike ride. "You get one when you get bigger."

"Me, too?" Brooke asked from her perch in a seat behind Val.

"Both of you do." Straddling her bike, Val squinted for a second up at the sky and the sun slipping behind a cloud. "Are we ready?"

Luke's eyes narrowed in her direction. "Check. It looks as if she unsnapped her helmet."

Val swung around with a few words to Brooke about not touching it. "Now we're ready," she said, looking at Luke. She noticed he was double-checking Traci's helmet, too. It was so typical of him. He took his car in early for oil changes and to have tires rotated. He stopped for gasoline when the gauge teetered at the halfway mark. He was a man who believed in preventive safety and good sense.

When she'd been in her last trimester of pregnancy, he'd take over the housecleaning and laundry, doing everything conceivable to safeguard the baby's and her health. Despite all those precautions, he hadn't been able to do enough.

"We're ready," he said.

Val tossed her head back to banish more sad thoughts from sneaking in. It was a day for fun. With a nod, they began pumping up a hill. Glancing up again, she eyed the sky darkening with pewter-colored clouds. "If it rains, remember this was your idea."

Grinning, Luke signaled her to turn right. "It was your idea."

"Not if it rains," she bantered back.

"It wouldn't dare," he said with snide amusement. "Tonight's Cindy's party. Doesn't she pray to the sun god or something on the morning of her parties?"

Val aimed a smile at him as they coasted down the hill. Cindy had had perfect weather at last year's party. Everything had seemed perfect to Val then.

She'd been enjoying the knowledge that she was pregnant. She'd just begun to show, and friends had greeted them with mommy and daddy jokes.

"Vali, go faster," Brooke said from behind her, cutting into her thoughts.

She pumped faster for a moment. What was wrong with her today? Why was she drawing up so much of the past suddenly? All that mattered was the present. She was with her husband and two little girls who'd won her heart from the first moment she'd seen them. Was the possibility of losing them drudging up old memories? No preagonizing today, she railed herself while braking for a curve. What good was there in worrying about the future, about possibilities that were far too painful?

With Luke's glance toward her, she saw a warmth in his eyes that had nothing to do with passion. We're going to be all right, she decided. All of us.

Luke left for his office within half an hour after they returned home.

"Me do it," Traci insisted as Val stacked their lunch dishes in the dishwasher.

Patiently Val waited while she completed the task. As usual, Traci switched from little helper to drummer in a second. Sitting on the floor, she happily banged a wooden spoon on several pots that she'd pulled from the cabinet.

Val loaded clothes into the dryer. As Brooke passed by, dangling one of Luke's shoes, she snatched it from her. "You can't take that shoe into the sandbox."

Her little mouth puffed to a pout before she stomped outside to the tractor tire filled with sand. Val considered her momentary displeasure a lot less to deal with than Luke's would be if he put on a shoe stuffed with sand.

With both girls not together, she sensed defeat in keeping an eye on them. Choosing her oldest pot and spoon, she led Traci toward her sister.

Plopped in the middle of the sand, Brooke poured it from one plastic container to another. As Traci scrambled in beside her, Brooke ladled some of the sand onto Traci's knee.

Val sensed what was coming next.

Traci scooped up a handful of sand and gleefully watched it stream between her fingers over the laces of Brooke's shoe.

Their squeals wafted on the air. Busy covering each other with sand, they didn't fight once. Goals bound people together. But she already knew that was true. Because of a determination to keep the girls, she and Luke were together again.

A rare occasion occurred that evening. Luke came home early enough for them to arrive at the party on time. Val considered burying his beeper under a mountain of pillows, but her conscience resisted.

While he called the hospital to check on several patients, she wandered into the bathroom and showered. One big question remained unanswered. Standing in front of her closet several minutes later, Val stalled in taking her dress from the hanger. ''Are you still going?'' she asked as Luke finally ambled into the bedroom. Often enough one phone call had changed their plans.

"Still going." He stripped off his shirt slowly, distracted by her wearing only an ivory-colored teddy. Sleek-looking, it emphasized her fragile slimness. With her bare shoulders and smooth back enticing him, he made a suggestion. "We could forget the party."

The intensity of the gaze moving over her in a slow, memorizing manner danced pleasure across her skin. "Too late to think about that." Laughter rose in her voice. "They'd ring our phone off the hook, wondering where we were."

Not to be dissuaded, Luke started to move closer to her. The twins' singing in the other room halted him. "They can't be awake already," he muttered more to himself than to her.

It was impossible for Val to ignore him as he flung his shirt onto a nearby chair and mumbled something under his breath. "Do you have a problem?"

In response to her airy tease, Luke stilled at the doorway. "Do you remember all the times the Russo sisters and their husbands joked about grabbing time in the afternoon while the kids napped?"

Val recalled several conversations about hit-and-miss romance with kids around. "I remember." Knowing the twins would tramp in soon, she slid on her robe.

His imagination still fully engaged, Luke braced a shoulder against the doorjamb. "It might be fun."

Val raised her eyes from the tie on her robe. "What might be?"

"Sneaking off with my wife," he said before closing the door behind him.

Amused, Val settled at her dressing table. After being so sure she'd never feel joy again, suddenly so much was with her. Brushing her hair, she smiled at the familiarity of the moment with him bellowing out his own version of "Chances Are" over the rush of running water. This was how it used to be. This was how it could always be.

At the patter of footsteps behind her, she paused in reaching for her eyeliner and raised her head. Her dressing table mirror reflected two grinning urchins on each side of her face. "Up from your naps?"

"Aw done." Brooke craned her neck to see the makeup on the dressing table.

Val swiped the blusher brush at the small nose.

"Let Traci see," her sister insisted.

Brooke beamed at her twin, then peered at herself in the mirror.

They both laughed as Val dabbed some on Traci's nose, too.

"Makeup," Brooke announced proudly at herself in the mirror.

Val recalled comments from others with teenage daughters and had no doubt a few arguments loomed in the future about the same subject.

Luke emerged from the bathroom to see the girls clumping around in Val's heels while she finished applying her makeup. "You'll never get ready at this rate." Lightly he passed a hand over Val's shoulder. "Come on, girls."

Val gave him merit points. Traci ran off with his shoes and Brooke chased her, dragging his tie.

After giving them a suitable headstart, Luke managed to overtake them at the bottom step and snagged his shoes and tie from little hands. "Where are your puzzles?"

"Me get," Brooke volunteered, and raced her sister to the box of toys. As large wooden pieces spilled onto the floor with their tug of war over them, she scowled down at the puzzles. "Uh-oh."

Unable to stop a grin, Luke dropped to their level. "Uh-oh, is right."

With a little coaxing, he managed to get the girls to pick up the puzzles and settle on the floor with them in front of the television set.

Zipping up her dress, Val stilled and listened. She heard nothing. From experience, she was learning to be more alert when the house got too quiet. Preparing for whatever, she peered over the railing.

Nothing could have prepared her.

On the carpet, Brooke was cross-legged while Traci sat lopsided with one leg tucked underneath her. Between them, Luke lay on his belly. Heads bent, the three of them concentrated on the giant puzzle pieces.

"Here?" Traci held a puzzle piece in her hand above an empty spot in the puzzle board.

"Here," he answered, tickling her ribcage.

In a fit of laughter, she fell into him. Rolling onto his back, he took her down with one arm and grabbed Brooke who'd pounced on him to join in the play.

Touched, Val stepped back from the sight of him holding two giggling little girls. A mellow warmth stayed with her while she finished dressing.

Neil and Cindy's rambling ranch was ablaze with lights. The chance for rain that had threatened earlier had disappeared, but a humid breeze rustled the leaves of the giant oaks bordering the driveway.

Strolling with Luke up the winding walkway to the house, Val couldn't resist a tease. "Did you have fun playing today?"

"Lord, they're exhausting." His lips curved in a wry grin. "How do you do it?"

"I am woman."

Luke gave her a slow once-over, his eyes sweeping down the cool blue, tea-length dress. She looked stunning. Unable to resist, he curled a hand over her hip intimately. "Yes, you definitely are."

Before they could ring the doorbell, Cindy was opening the door. Her dimples winking at them, she was dressed in a sparkling green cocktail dress. "You're fashionably on time," she said lightly as she ushered them to the backyard.

Twice a year, Cindy and Neil threw the town's best barbecues. The one earlier in the summer had included swimming, hamburgers and hot dogs, corn on the cob and the usual picnic fare, plus volleyball and swimming for the kids. Their Autumn bash was formal, parents only, complete with appetizers, a catered buffet dinner plus Neil's specialty—cornish hens roasting on the spit—dancing, and white-jacketed college students serving champagne.

With her hand in Luke's, Val wandered with him past Cindy's prize-winning rosebushes to a stone walkway that led to the pool area and beyond that a fruit orchard.

"She spent four days in Dallas shopping," Fred Henderson said about his wife to the couple beside them, "while I sat in a stuffy conference room."

"Wonderful trip," his wife chirped between sips of champagne.

Val smiled at their easy banter after twenty years of marriage.

Subdued male laughter drifted from the area around the giant barbecue pit that Neil had built himself, something he never failed to remind anyone who'd listen. Watching Pricilla Barrington's love, Jake Spencer, cock his cowboy hat and distractedly glance away, Val guessed that Neil was explaining his brick-by-brick labors. Since mingling was always the game plan at Cindy's parties, Val chose the best person, in her opinion, to do that with. "I'm going over by Jenny," she said after locating her near the pool talking to Pricilla.

Luke made eye contact with Mitch McCord who looked trapped in conversation with Barbara Fleming, the mayor's wife. He read Mitch's silent message to be rescued. "Don't wander too far." He gave her hand a gentle squeeze. "Neil seems to have hired a decent band this year. I'd like to dance."

The smile in his eyes looked the same way in the soft light of morning when they were filled with passion. "I'll save the first for you."

"And the last."

As his hand brushed her arm, Val stroked his cheek. "I always leave with the man I come with," she said with a seductive promise before breezing out of his arm's length.

Chatter circled the yard beneath the sparkling Italian lights strung along the patio and the outside of white canopies. Val inched her way past couples, answering their greetings.

The moment she drew near, Jenny snagged her arm. "Everyone is talking about your grandfather."

Lord, now what? On other occasions, he'd raised his fists and challenged one teenager who'd been rude to the minister's wife, he'd gotten a megaphone and had declared to anyone who'd listened that a body shop owner who'd quoted one price to him had overcharged him.

"Excuse me," Pricilla piped in. "But my honey definitely needs help," she said about Jake.

"I overheard," Cindy suddenly said. "Are you talking about Edwin and Myrna Traynor?"

"Who isn't?" Jenny answered, scooting Val along by the elbow as Cindy urged her toward the buffet table.

Surveying the table burdened with food, Val chose a shrimp hors d'oeuvre. She thought everyone was jumping to conclusions about her grandfather and Myrna.

"I have it on good authority that Myrna is having a romantic dinner with him tonight," Cindy said speculatively, and looked at Val for confirmation. "Beatrice Elwood and Adelaide Simpson are green with envy."

"Who is the good authority?" Val asked, wondering who was gossiping about her grandfather.

"Agnes, Minny and Ethel."

Jenny released an unladylike snort.

Val, too, had her doubts about the accuracy of their gossip. Though she found it difficult to believe that her grandfather had changed feelings he'd maintained about her grandmother since she'd died ten years ago, she'd like to believe he was truly interested in Myrna.

Cindy swiveled her head away for a second, then leaned conspiratorially close. "I think they're perfect for each other," she declared.

Munching on a crisp, miniature spring roll, Jenny stretched for a cocktail napkin. "Who? Myrna and Val's grandfather?"

"Oh, I hope so, but I meant Michael and Michelle. Valerie should know." Cindy pointed in the direction of a spinach dip. "You must try this."

Val looked past colleagues of Luke's who were intense in their discussion. Michael and Michelle stood with their heads bent toward each other as they shared a laugh. She could remember easily now the time when she and Luke had been so in love that no one else existed. "What should I know?" she asked in regard to Cindy's comment.

"You have the perfect marriage, so you'd be the best judge."

Deceit never set well with Val. *We sure had you all fooled,* she mused. With their expectant looks, she shrugged. "What can anyone tell about another couple."

"Everyone always could tell that you and Lucas were wonderful together," Cindy insisted.

Val had always considered herself quick-witted enough to dodge the most uncomfortable moments. "You could describe a lot of people in this town that way. What about Pricilla and Jake?"

They stared for only a second as if thinking, then nodded in unison.

Affectionately, Val nudged Jenny with an elbow. "Or you and Mitch?"

Jenny beamed. "She has a point. We are perfect together."

Along with Cindy, Val laughed. Across the room she saw Neil bending Luke's ear about something. His head turned, his eyes capturing hers as she sank her teeth into the hors d'oeuvre. Her blood warmed with a look, one she never had trouble reading. He wanted them to be alone.

"Oh, my." The tease edging Cindy's voice grabbed Val's attention. "You two sometimes still act like a just-married couple," she said about the lengthy stare Val had shared with Luke. "I suppose when a marriage is so good, the honeymoon never ends."

"It will now," Barbara Fleming interrupted, joining them. "There is no way you're going to play lovebirds with a set of two-year-olds running around."

"They are everywhere," Val admitted. "It's amazing the energy they have."

Barbara tipped her head curiously. "Do you have the new mother syndrome?"

"What's that?" Val asked, reaching for another shrimp.

"Tired, tired, tired."

"Luke helps a lot," she murmured between chews, and thought to ask Cindy about the crabmeat stuffing. "So it's not too hard on me."

"Having someone does help," Barbara murmured, her voice dropping to a whisper. "I don't know what poor Faith Harper will do. Being alone and pregnant."

Another exchange with Jenny was all that was needed to know they were of one mind. After so many years of friendship, sometimes words didn't need to be said. Jenny was as uncomfortable as Val was about gossip regarding Faith.

"Have you seen Faith recently?" Cindy asked, also not seeming inclined to appease Barbara's gossipy nature.

Val shot a look at Jenny. Neither of them had seen nor talked to Faith yesterday. "I saw her two weeks ago at Wendy Wilcox's house," Val went on, hoping to direct the conversation down a more positive path. "And when Faith left, we mentioned a baby shower for her."

"That's a good idea." Cindy paused one of the white-jacketed men serving champagne and handed a fluted glass to Val. "You don't have one of these." She took a glass for herself before going on. "We should show Faith that her friends are behind her."

"Yes, a good idea," Barbara replied, but looked away.

If she wanted to find someone to gossip with and who'd be less loyal to Faith, Val could have told her that she wouldn't find that person at the party.

Having wound a path toward the buffet table, Luke stood only feet away now and was deep in conversation with the mayor.

Jenny's soft giggle drew Val's attention back to her. "I bet Luke is being hustled into playing the piano at this year's annual club talent show."

Watching Luke's expression turn more serious, Val gave Jenny only a semblance of a smile. Something else was being discussed. A flicker of worry knit Luke's brow for a second.

"Valerie, is something wrong?"

By Jenny's question, she realized she was frowning. "I don't know. But I plan to find out." Stepping away, she inched her way past Travis Donovan talking to the mayor's visiting niece and sidestepped a group gathered around Michael and Michelle. As she neared Luke, his gaze met hers. Val smiled at Morten Fleming, the town's mayor.

Silver hair crowned a face with soft features and sparkling eyes. "I would have called you with this news," Morten was saying, "but I didn't learn about it until minutes before I was ready to leave for the party. When I called your house, Irene said you'd already left. So I thought I'd share what I've been hearing when I saw you here. Nothing definite, you understand."

Instinctively Val slipped her hand in Luke's.

"Morten saw the state worker's initial report about us," he said as an explanation.

The mayor beamed. "She wrote that the Dawson twins are right where they belong."

Val felt a bubble of pleasure sweep through her. "That's wonderful."

"She said that unless her study uncovers something unexpected, she couldn't see any reason why the girls shouldn't stay where they'll be happiest. Where they are right now," he added.

Val barely restrained her elation.

"So I'm glad to say that it really looks good for you two."

"Thanks, Morten, for telling us." Luke felt her shift against him.

"Glad to do it." He looked somewhat amused. "So what is it like, being parents to those youngsters?"

Luke thought of the toilet paper trail, the overflowing toilet, the endless nighttime rituals. "Interesting. Fun," he admitted. Despite all the work, not a day went by without laughter.

Val felt easier about expressing her true feelings to others now. "They are wonderful," Val said. "They follow me everywhere. And Traci loves imitating tasks. We dust together. And Brooke joined Luke while he shaved the other morning. She used her toothbrush."

Morten chuckled. "You sound like proud parents." In a gesture that denoted friendship more than political graciousness, he closed his hands over Val's. "Everyone is behind you."

Val answered with another thank you. Morten had said something similar at Kelly's funeral. Too close to letting sad memories slip in, Val curled an arm around Luke's back. "How about that dance?"

With her hand in his, Luke zigzagged a path around clusters of people and led her onto the small platform of a gazebo set up for dancing.

The night air whispered across Val's bare arms with an unnatural warmth for October. When Luke gathered her in his arms, she rested her cheek against his face. "This has to make a difference," she said, unable to contain her excitement. "If we're recommended, then why would they give the twins to Charlene?"

Pulling back, he saw a glow on her face, a brightness in her eyes that had been gone for so long. Dancing seemed too public suddenly. "Let's walk," he urged, wanting to be alone with her and away from the party. Not letting her go, he led her toward the orchard at the back of the property.

A sliver of moon peeked out from behind clouds in the dark sky. When he slowed their stride near a trellis of ivy, Val couldn't stand another moment. Happiness humming through her, she flung her arms around his neck.

Her pleasure seeping into him, Luke tugged her so close to him that they had to breathe as one. "We need to celebrate."

A firm believer in celebrating even the smallest joys, Val deepened the kiss. What was a better reason than becoming a family? "What do you suggest?" she murmured beneath his lips.

Luke smiled against her cheek now. "A glass of wine, candlelight—you," he answered softly. Never did he want to see the smile in her eyes fade again. "Did I tell you that you look beautiful?"

"Yes." She laughed, pleased, and framed his face with her hands to bring his mouth close once more.

Capturing her lips beneath his, Luke wondered if he'd ever get enough of her. An urgency swept through him that he knew couldn't be satiated. Yet he kissed her until he ached, until he was certain all that he felt caressed every fiber of her.

Feeling limp, Val clung to his shoulders. "That was—"

"Great," he said on an uneven breath, and buried his face in her hair.

"Unexpected."

"You started it."

Val toyed with a button on his shirt. "How did I do that?"

"You touched me."

"You're easy," she teased, kissing a corner of the mouth that had just given her so much pleasure.

"With you. Always."

As his fingers caressed the back of her neck, igniting another small fire inside her, she released a long breath. "Luke, what are we doing?"

"Falling in love," he whispered.

She felt her insides soften. Meeting the eyes searching hers for confirmation, she knew now that she never wanted them to break up. "We could make this work, couldn't we?"

Luke realized he desperately needed all the words from her. "You've changed your mind?"

He couldn't be resisting. Unsure, she strove for a tease. "Are you trying to confuse me?"

The blue eyes remained deadly serious. "Trying to make sure."

One of them had to take the first step. As his hand shifted to the sharp angle of her hip, she touched his cheek. "I love you. I never stopped loving you."

Time seemed to stop. He kissed her brow, then her temple. She loved him again. He'd make sure nothing changed that this time. No more mistakes. "And I love you," he said on a whisper.

With those words echoing in her head, her lips sought his for a long, endless moment. There would be a lot of moments for them now, Val thought, clinging to him. Even though his mouth lifted from hers, she felt his body heating beneath her hands at his chest. He was as caught up in the moment as she was. "We'd better stop." The sound of the music and the buzz of conversation from the party reached her again and she arched away from the moist heat of his lips trailing down the side of her neck.

Desire darkening his eyes, he ran a fingertip slowly down her cheek. "Only for now."

"Excuse me." Those words and a distinct clearing of the throat forced them apart. Standing in the shadows, Neil peered over the rim of his glasses at them. "You're going to have to tell everyone your secret," he said, sounding amused.

Luke turned Val with him to return to the party. "What secret?"

"How you keep the fire going after all these years?"

A laugh flowed up from Val's throat. "Fan it."

Chapter Eleven

The faint light of dawn streamed into the room between the slats of the venetian blinds on the bedroom window. Her eyes half closed, Val scooted closer to Luke and bent her head to kiss his chest.

"That's some good morning," he murmured in a husky morning voice. It amazed him, but he burned for her. Despite a loving night, he wanted her again, yearned to see the sensuous softness in her eyes. As she nestled closer, her scent filled him. She was all he remembered and more. Last night, she'd enticed him to the point where he'd trembled with sensations.

"I wish we could stay here all day," she whispered in a lazy manner in his ear.

"Fat chance with the dynamic duo running around." His eyes closing again, he set his jaw against the top of her head as she rested it on his chest.

"They did learn to climb out of their cribs fast, didn't they?"

Luke skimmed the roundness of her hip. "Do you hear anything right now?"

Angling her face toward him, she kissed the base of his throat. "Nothing."

The scent of her was so much a part of him. With an easy roll, he trapped her beneath him.

A soft giggle slipped from Val's throat. "Is this going to be one of those quickies that old married couples with kids whisper about?"

"Not too quick," he answered, lowering his mouth to her breast.

The girls tramped from their bedroom to the bathroom to watch Luke as he finished shaving. With a few minutes to herself before breakfast, Val dumped clothes in the washing machine, then started filling the sink with water for the breakfast dishes. The sound of Brooke's yelling drifted to her. Val pushed down the faucet handle to stop the water. Before whatever was happening escalated into a war, she followed the sound of Brooke's voice.

Standing on a ladder to change a light bulb in the foyer, Luke looked amused.

With her teddy bear dangling in her hand, Brooke stood at the bottom of the ladder and was pointing a scolding finger at him. "Get down."

"Hey. You're two. I'm thirty-six," he reminded her.

Her bow-shaped mouth puckered with disapproval. "Tell, Vali." She whirled around, yelling, "Vali! Vali!"

"I'm right here." Val barely veiled her amusement. She wondered if he remembered that he'd said the exact same words to Brooke when she'd been on the counter. "He's big. He can do that."

"Me, too?"

Val rolled her eyes. She should have known she'd be pulled in to such a discussion. "No, you're too small."

Descending the ladder, Luke spotted the glow-in-the-dark bandage slapped on the teddy bear's leg. "What happened to Bear?" he asked to sidetrack her.

Little arms lifted the teddy bear to him to be kissed. "Ow-ee."

Luke did as was expected and planted one on the fuzzy leg.

Val turned away quickly. "Coffee's made."

He'd have sworn he heard her snort of laughter. He handed the teddy bear back to Brooke and smiled. Being the brunt of Val's amusement seemed like a small price to pay to see her so happy again. With the rich aroma of coffee beckoning him, he ushered the girls into the kitchen.

Standing at the sink with her back to him, Val held the telephone receiver and assured the caller, "Yes, I'll meet you there around that time."

Luke ambled to the coffee brewer. By her easy tone, he assumed the caller was Jenny or Wendy or one of her other friends. "Where are you headed?"

"The Baby Boutique."

She said it with a casualness that made Luke breathe easier. For a few months after Kelly had died, they couldn't drive past Faith's store without tears swimming in Val's eyes. Healing. They were both healing now. "Have you seen my new tie?"

"Nope." She noticed he'd left his collar open, and an old tie, a favorite of his, stuck out of his pants' pocket. Though Brooke was concentrating on cornering the last of the doughnut-shaped cereal with her spoon, in the nearby high chair, Traci stared down at her spoon floating in the milk. "That was Jenny on the phone. She said there's a carnival in town." Val waited until Brooke finished, then took the cereal bowl from her. "She noticed a lot of rides for little ones and..."

"We could go after I come home." Luke noted her eyes smiled almost all the time now.

"That would be fun."

"Down. Luke, down," Traci insisted from behind him.

He swung toward her to lift her from her high chair, but stilled, letting her stand in the chair while he fingered his new tie draped around her waist. "Where did you get this?"

"Pretty."

"Yeah, I thought so." Despite his deadpan look, Val saw laughter in his eyes.

Gently he lowered her to the floor, then accommodated Brooke's request to get out of her high chair. When he turned away from them, Val blocked his path.

"About tonight," he said when she placed her hands on the strong planes of his face.

A teasing spirit swept over her. "Early tonight? Or late tonight?"

"Early tonight. We already know what we're doing late tonight."

Damp from his shower, his dark hair shone with faint red highlights. "Do you want to have dinner first before we go to the carnival?" she asked, touching the strands at the nape of his neck.

Luke gave her credit. Tomorrow was the big day— the court hearing. He didn't doubt her thoughts had strayed with a mound of what-ifs, but she was keeping her spirit light. "I'd rather go out."

Val leaned back against his arm to give him a thoughtful look. "Where?"

He kissed her nose. "You look adorable."

"Definitely," she said on a laugh, because she hadn't taken time to do more than run her fingers through her hair. "What do you want to eat?"

"Hamburgers, hot dogs," he said, aware of what her reaction would be.

She was predictable. "You're an incorrigible influence."

Releasing her, he bent and put his face in front of Traci who was chatting on her play phone to an imaginary caller. "Do you like hot dogs?"

"Hot dog." Her face lit with a smile.

"Brooke?" Luke waited until she eased her attention from spinning a dial on an activity table. "Hot dog?"

She grinned. "Yum."

Laughter danced in his eyes. "There you are. They approve. It's unanimous."

Of course the girls had agreed. And that was what he'd wanted—to please them.

"I'll see you later." He kissed Traci, then Brooke.

Despite the two-year-olds staring up at them, he moved toward Val with a tease sparkling in his eyes and backed her up toward the counter.

Coiling her arms around his neck, she laughed. "I like your style, Doc."

Wanting to surprise the girls with new clothes, Val dropped them off at Irene's, then drove to the Baby Boutique, eager to see Faith.

In the window of the store, the softly tinted lights overhead shone on a new display, this time of holiday dresses. Val inched toward the second window, which Faith had devoted to the display of toys.

Skimming several famous Disney character squeezies, a Sesame Street tape recorder, a few stuffed animals and an easel desk, she thought the desk might be perfect for the twins since it could be drawn on from both sides.

Through the window, she saw Faith behind the counter, manning the cash register. Though almost eight months pregnant, she seemed so slender everywhere else. Faith's long brown hair shone. Val remembered during her own pregnancy that her hair had been dull and wondered what her friend's secret was. The only customer inside was Wendy Wilcox, the postmistress, looking smug about something and chatting with Faith.

Noting that Faith's smile didn't reach her eyes, Val couldn't recall when a sadness had begun to dull them. She remembered the February engagement party for Michael and Michelle at Faith's house. Faith had seemed all right. Val sighed. What did she know? She'd barely been functioning. An obligation to share hostess duties with Wendy and Faith had forced her to go.

It had been a difficult time for her. She'd lost Kelly in February, only weeks before the party, but she'd braved the crowd, plastering a smile on her face at appropriate moments, not wanting to spoil Michael and Michelle's happiness. By the time she'd driven home that night, she'd felt like collapsing from the strain of looking happy when all she'd wanted to do was weep.

That time seemed long ago suddenly. Shifting her thoughts to turtlenecks and jumpers, she stepped in. Above her, a soft bell rang.

Wendy whirled around and immediately grinned. "Valerie, hi. I can't believe you're alone. Where are the twins?"

"With Irene." Val crossed the ceramic tile and the plush, pale gray carpet to bridge the distance to the counter. "I came the other day, but the store was closed."

Faith stacked several receipts. "I let Beth have the day off, so she could do some extra studying. And I had to drive in to Dallas to see a doctor."

All of her worry about Faith with her again, Val inched closer. "Faith, there's nothing wrong, is there?" she asked.

"No." A slip of a smile curved Faith's lips. "Dr. Austin suggested I go, though, for another ultrasound because my blood pressure went up a little. But everything was normal. He said so this morning."

Val nodded with relief.

As Faith turned away to hang a dress on a rack, Wendy sidled closer. "Valerie, would Dr. Austin tell Lucas if something was wrong?" she whispered.

"He might tell Luke, but Luke wouldn't tell me because of doctor-patient confidentiality," Valerie answered, then shook her head. "But I don't think anything is wrong."

"Except..." Wendy said in a low voice.

Before reaching for two jumpers, Val exchanged a quick, concerned look with her. All of Faith's friends wished they could help her. But she was reticent to talk about the baby's father—to anyone.

"Valerie, what did you want to see?" Faith asked, skirting the counter.

Val pointed to the jumpers on the nearby rack. "Those." She laughed at herself. "I came for play clothes," she said while choosing several turtlenecks and slip-on pants for the twins. "But those dresses in the window are so adorable."

"Faith, you're going to have a big sale today," Wendy gibed while fingering one yellow turtleneck.

Val took her tease good-naturedly. "Traci will love that pink one." She'd chosen the yellow for Brooke, remembering how often she chose a yellow crayon when coloring. "What's in the bag?" Val asked, gesturing toward the one Wendy's hand was tightly gripping. "Weight-lifting equipment?"

"Books." Wendy set the bag down and retrieved the top book. Val tipped her head to read the title before Wendy announced, "This is *How To Hook A Husband.* I'm on a husband hunt."

Amused, Val draped a friendly arm around her shoulder. "Tell me. Who are you hunting? Is Travis Donovan on your list of potential husbands?"

Turning her face away, Wendy fingered a toddler-size cranberry velvet dress. "This one is pretty."

Val nodded agreeably. "I thought so. Are you avoiding answering me?"

Wendy swung a smile back at her. "No. He's gorgeous, and he sure has a sweet son," she said with warm affection for the five-year-old boy. "But my neighbor is antimarriage. Did you forget that?"

Everyone who knew Travis was aware of his views about marriage. "Your charm might change his mind."

"Forget it," Wendy answered. "There are plenty of other men."

"So," Val said, truly interested, "how do you go about husband hunting?"

Wendy picked up her bag again. "I plan to find out. That's why I have these—self-help books and magazines with articles about how to be sexier. I'm going to study them."

"Happy hunting," Val said with encouragement, and set the clothes that had caught her eye on the counter by Faith.

"Let me see the book," Faith requested, showing the same inquisitiveness as Val had. "Are you really going to do all this, Wendy?"

"That's my plan. November is my deadline," Wendy said with steely determination.

Val looked up from retrieving her wallet out of her shoulder bag. "For what?"

"I plan to be engaged before Michael and Michelle's wedding in November. Now, I've gotta run." And with a quick wave goodbye she headed out of the store.

Faith stared after Wendy's departing figure. Looking down, she began to bag Val's purchases.

Val waited for Faith to say how much she owed, but she was silent, keeping her head bowed—too long. Quickly Val rounded the counter to reach her. "Faith?" As she raised her head, Val saw the tears in Faith's blue eyes. "Oh, Faith, what's wrong?"

With a shake of her head, she started to step around Val. "I'll get Beth to finish this, Valerie."

Val cast a quick glance around for Beth then reached forward and touched Faith's arm. "Faith, please tell me what's wrong."

Val noticed Faith's hand went protectively to her swollen belly but reminded herself that Faith had said the baby was okay.

Taking a tissue from the pocket of her maternity smock, Faith dabbed the wetness from her cheeks. "The man—he..."

Val didn't want to pry but how could she walk away with Faith so upset? "Are you talking about the man who fathered your baby?"

Faith nodded, shoving the tissue back into her pocket.

Val scurried to the chair near the counter that Faith had brought into the shop for days when standing too long on her feet made them ache. "Do you want to sit?"

"No." Faith straightened her shoulders and raised her chin a notch. "He's married."

Val's voice raised. "Married? You didn't tell me he was a married man."

"He wasn't. When . . . when we were together, he wasn't."

Val zeroed in on what Faith was having so much trouble saying. "He got married?"

"Yes," Faith said softly. "I learned he got married soon after our night—our night together."

"Honey, who is he?" Val touched her arm. "He should know about you—about the baby."

Shaking her head, Faith took a step back. "No." She whirled away from Val before she could say more and rushed into the back room.

Seconds later, Beth emerged from the back room to bag Val's purchases. Her loyalty to Faith made her pretend nothing was wrong. She smiled at Val before she left the store.

Meeting Jenny outside the store, Val relayed what had happened and shared with Jenny a promise to keep an eye on Faith, then loaded her bags into the trunk of her car. An empty sensation lodged inside her as she drove toward Irene's to pick up the twins. It was clear that Faith was unhappy about a love that might never be, Wendy was wanting love so much she was willing to do anything, and she, too, was clinging to a love that had been and that she prayed truly lasted this time.

"Cake. Traci do it," Traci yelled to Luke when he came in the back door that evening.

In passing, Luke kissed Val's cheek, then closed the distance to the table and eyed the two-layer, chocolate cake they'd baked for the picnic. "It looks good."

As the girls beamed at him, he sent Val an amused grin. "Frosting has been short-changed, though, hasn't it?"

Grinning, she tipped her head to eye the bare side of the cake. "They both had to clean out the bowl."

"More went in the bowl than on the cake."

"That's why you're such a good doctor," Val teased. "You always see beyond the obvious."

Brooke tugged on his pant leg. "Let's go."

"We'll go as soon as I change," he promised. With the girls trailing him up the stairs to the bedroom and jabbering excitedly about the carnival, he stripped off his shirt.

"Soon?" Brooke asked.

"Yes, soon. Now out." He scooted them from the bedroom so he could change into his jeans. While yanking them up, he heard the twins outside the door, waiting for him. With a glance around, he wondered where his sneakers were. On his hands and knees, he eyed one under the bed and stretched for it.

"No, you stay out here," he heard Val say before the door opened.

From his position under the bed, all he could see were her feet.

"What are you doing?"

"Looking for my second sneaker." After inching out backward, he raised the shoe in the air like a trophy. "Found it." His voice trailed off and his eyes narrowed as he stared into the sneaker.

Val grimaced, guessing what was wrong. The adage that a picture was worth a thousand words seemed to suit the moment. With two fingers, he reached into his shoes then let the sand inside slip from his fingers back into it. "Whose idea was that sandbox?"

"Yours." Val backed out of the room, deciding she'd let him cool off by himself. She ushered the girls downstairs in case he spewed a few words unfit for young ears.

In the kitchen, she wrapped up several carrot sticks, and packed them and bananas into the basket. Hot dogs might be Luke's idea of a great dinner, but not hers.

No longer looking so grumpy, Luke raced the girls to the car. During the drive to the carnival, they dutifully nodded their heads to his lecture that shoes didn't belong in their sandbox.

Certain his mood was congenial, Val filled him in on what had happened at the Baby Boutique.

Disbelief edged his voice in response to her summary of Wendy's husband hunt campaign. "She *is* kidding?"

"No. She was serious." Val checked on the girls. Content in their car seats, they were talking to each other and their favorite dolls. "What do you think about Faith?" Val asked, still concerned for her friend.

"I think she's strong, but being alone, she has a tough time ahead."

Satisfied, Val nodded and eyed the crowd gathered in New Hope Park. "I meant to tell you earlier. Gramps called before you came home. He and Myrna will be at the carnival."

Luke let his attention drift from traffic as he braked at a stop sign. "He's still seeing her?"

"He was making dinner for them. And he wanted to know if I thought white candles would be okay."

"A romantic evening at seventy-one." He chuckled. "The man has class."

A setting sun glared off the chrome of the Ferris wheel when they strolled from the gravel parking lot. Smoke flowed up from the barbecue grills that people had lugged to the park. Balloons danced on the breeze. The sound of music floated on the air accompanied by the hand-clapping and feet-stomping audience that was watching the local square dancing group performing on a nearby platform.

In line for tickets, Luke held on tightly to Traci's hand, while Val kept Brooke's snug in her own. Dancing in place, Brooke impatiently tugged on Val's hand to hurry her toward the merry-go-round.

After pocketing the tickets, Luke scooped each girl up into an arm. Excitedly they chattered in his ears before he set each of them on one of the painted horses. When little hands were wrapped firmly around a pole, Val sidled close to Traci while Luke took a place beside Brooke. The soft, swaying beat of a waltz wafted through the air as the ride's whirling motion began.

"Whee, horsey," Traci yelled, delight dancing in her eyes.

Three rides later, they scurried toward the trill of the toy train. While they scrambled into seats, Luke lounged against a nearby post and munched on a bag of popcorn he'd bought. "They're going to wear us out."

Relaxing against him, Val slipped an arm around his back. "You're getting old, Doc."

Even faster, he thought, since they'd become parents of rambunctious toddlers.

When the ride ended, the twins raced toward the miniature car of their choice. Clanging the bell on her fire engine, Traci abandoned the steering wheel to wave as she drove by. The always more sedate Brooke had chosen a police car, but her siren wailed whenever she passed them.

"Where are the little ones?" Val's grandfather said from behind them.

Val didn't bother answering.

His gaze had already shifted to the twins. "Sweet, aren't they, Myrna?" he murmured almost proudly to the woman standing beside him.

Looking like a man ten years younger, he gave Val an ear-splitting smile as he introduced Myrna to her and Luke. "Smart," he said low to Luke about Myrna when she was engaged in conversation with Val about the town's upcoming annual cook-off. "And a good cook. She knows how to treat a man. Made me chicken and rice and a *butter* sauce."

Val discerned that Myrna had also overheard him.

She sent Val a discreet wink. "I always cook low-fat, low-cholesterol. It's healthier for everyone. He said he couldn't tell, so the food was all right."

Val kept a thought to herself. For her stubborn grandfather to make such a concession, he must be in love.

As people milled around, searching for a place on the grass, Val hurried to the gazebo. While the twins

staked a spot, she was stopped once by Pricilla. Val
assured her that she'd seen Faith.

"Going to keep an eye on that gal," Pricilla commented before walking away.

That sounded like a good idea to Val, too.

With the girls' help, Val spread out a blanket while
Luke bought the hot dogs for the twins and hamburgers for him and Val. Seeing him with hands full, maneuvering his way to them, she bounded to a stand to
help.

"Everyone in town must be here," he muttered
while handing her the twins' hot dogs.

"Grumble, grumble," she teased. "You exagger-
ate," she said, and nearly plowed into a young boy
chasing a Frisbee.

"Did that make my point?" he asked, shielding her
to prevent a group of teenagers who were busy flirt-
ing and talking from bumping into her and knocking
the dinner out of her hands.

Val's low laugh drifted over him when they dropped
onto the blanket beside the girls.

Looking up from digging into the picnic basket, she
wasn't unaware that the eyes staring at her were serious, warm, steady. "Want something?"

Luke arched a brow. "What a question." Ridicu-
lously while she knelt and unpacked a picnic basket,
and two toddlers zoomed around her, pretending to be
airplanes, a flicker of desire rushed through him.
Blocking thoughts that weren't fit for a picnic and the
company of two-year-olds, he braced his back against
the sturdy trunk of a huge oak.

Val offered him a can of soda. "The first picnic we
went on was more romantic than this."

Luke recalled a dash to a nearby barn, humid air, and a kiss that made him ache as if he were sixteen again. A lot of days and a lot of kisses had passed since then. He'd thought he would never love her more than he had on that day. He'd been wrong. Seeing her in the role of a mother, he realized how much he'd taken for granted, how special, how caring she was. "This is romantic," he finally answered.

She gave him an interested stare, wondering how he'd come to that conclusion.

"Sort of." Luke bent his leg and held the soda can on his knee. "How many men go on a picnic with three pretty women?"

Her eyes danced with a smile. "Smooth."

"More pickles, pease," Traci insisted while examining the hot dog Luke had just set in her hand.

Val peeled the pickles off her hamburger and loaded them on Traci's hot dog.

As Luke opened his mouth to take a bite of his hamburger, Brooke crawled closer and studied him somberly. He slanted a look at her. "Do you want more pickles, too?"

Brooke wagged her head. "Pee, pee."

"Perfect timing," Val said lightly, and pushed to her feet, offering Brooke her hand. "Come on."

"Traci, too," Traci insisted, and scrambled to a stand.

Val looked down to see Luke happily munching on his hamburger. "The least you could do is not look so comfortable."

"I'm just glad they're girls and not boys."

Laughing, Val braced her hands on his shoulders, then kissed him.

This is what they should always have had. His gaze stayed with Val and the girls, walking away hand-in-hand. This was what they'd expected. Two people in love with a family of their own.

Chapter Twelve

Luke stripped off his operating scrubs. The patient was recovering in ICU, his condition stable. Luke had left word at the nurse's station where he could be reached, but he'd already consulted with the doctor in the emergency room about the patient's condition. Foreseeing no complications, the man would be headed home by the end of the week.

Luke snatched up his sports coat and, hooking it on a finger, flung it over his shoulder. He passed the nurse's station on the way to the elevator.

"Good luck today," one of them offered.

Everyone knew. Dr. Lucas Kincaid and his wife were scheduled for a court battle today. Luke forced a confident grin and headed for the elevator. A few steps from it, another doctor flagged him down. More words of encouragement, wishes of good luck. If only that was all it would take.

As he always did on these early morning trips home, he stopped at his mother's. Her coffee seemed stronger today. "Any more news from your youngest son?"

"He phoned to tell me that I should remind you of something. Kincaids are winners."

Luke thought his brother still a touch naive if he believed that always held true.

"Who's taking care of the twins when you're in court?"

Luke rubbed a hand across tired eyes. He'd have to snag a few hours' sleep before their court appearance. "Myrna volunteered to sit with them."

"I would, but Harry wants me in court."

"I know, Mom. This is okay. The twins know Myrna."

She nodded as if giving her approval. Her hands toyed with her spoon until it was perfectly lined up with a square in the plaid tablecloth.

She needed assurances, just as Val would, Luke realized. "I think we should take the girls out for ice cream after the court hearing today."

Lifting her head, she met his stare with eyes that sparkled. "That's a good idea." She fed on his confidence about the day's outcome. "Why don't we have a small celebration here? We could invite over anyone who comes to court to support you and Valerie."

He thought they'd both be exhausted from the emotional strain. "Sounds great, Mom."

As she stood with him, he gave her a hug and his best grin. Only when he reached his car did he allow his own uncertainties to slip in. He wasn't sure if by the end of the day, he might lose more than the twins. They'd brought him and Val together. Without them, would they drift apart again?

Since awakening, Val had been trying to pretend this was a day like any other. The tremors in her stomach reminded her that it wasn't. So many things could happen in court today. The judge might give them final guardianship of the twins. Or Charlene's lawyer might present enough of a legitimate complaint that they'd still have only temporary custody and be faced with a custody battle. Or they might lose the girls.

Val shut her eyes at the thought. She couldn't allow that one to take hold. The girls jabbered, playing with their teacups and dolls before and after breakfast. With Luke at the hospital for a few hours, she was in desperate need of adult conversation. On a heavy sigh, she poured her third cup of coffee, though it wasn't even seven o'clock yet, then dialed Jenny's number.

"You're lucky you called me or I'd have beat your door down," Jenny said on a laugh after their greeting.

Val clung to the amusement in her friend's voice as if it were a lifeline. "What's the emergency?"

"A four-alarm blaze."

"What?"

"What else could it be?" Jenny teased. "I saw the way you and Luke looked at each other Saturday night. That wasn't part of any act, was it? Something is definitely happening?"

"Yes." Val tried to mask her uneasiness about what she might have to face today. "We're living in chaos, but everything is wonderful."

Jenny had been too close of a friend for too long. "You never lie and for good reason. You're lousy at it."

"Okay. I'm worried, Jenny." Val spoke the fear in her heart. "Over and over, I keep thinking. What if Charlene wins? She doesn't know that Traci sheds her shoes and socks whenever she enters the house, or seen her hug her books about horses, or is aware that Brooke is a chow-hound who will eat anything except green vegetables and loves playing with her toy computer." Val realized that all sounded so trivial, but it was important for stability in the girls' lives.

"She won't get them. The judge will see how much you love them."

"It isn't important that I want them. What matters is their happiness. How can they be happy with someone who doesn't want to know them? So I keep telling myself that we have to be the ones who get them."

"You will."

Val knew she'd go crazy if she believed differently. "Thanks for listening to me. I'll talk to you again after this is over."

"No, you won't. I'll be there today," Jenny assured her before saying goodbye.

Val hooked the receiver back in its cradle. Nothing helped to stop her mind from dwelling on today's court hearing. They'd turned in tax returns and medical histories. Val didn't doubt the state worker had also contacted police to check for criminal activities. What the stack of papers didn't show was how comfortable the twins were with them or how much they loved the girls.

Lost in thoughts, she slowly turned toward the telephone and wondered how long it had been ringing. Revving up a bright sound, she offered a greeting.

"Valerie?"

"Gramps, hi." He was speaking, but his words weren't completely registering. Mentally she shook her head.

"So will you come over?" he asked. "It's important."

"Is something wrong?"

"Nothing. Nothing at all."

She'd swear she heard a smile in his voice.

"I wouldn't have bothered you today," he said when she and the twins strolled into his kitchen a few minutes later. "I know you have the court hearing to think about."

Actually she was grateful for a diversion. "I'm glad you did call." Unpacking the girls' coloring books, she noticed her grandfather had set dishes on the kitchen counter.

"Well, anyway," he said, "I wouldn't have called you, but the minister reminded me this morning that the church rummage sale is this coming weekend. I could pack all this myself, but I'd be up all night."

Val thought he was exaggerating and believed he had another reason for asking her over. "So why did you decide to get rid of all this now?"

"I've been hanging on to it for too long. Your grandmother would say I was acting like a silly, sentimental old fool. She'd be right."

"I wouldn't call you that." Aware the twins were investigating his cupboards for something to get into, she raised a halting hand to him. "I'll be right back."

She ushered the girls into his living room and delivered a brief lecture about not touching anything before she rejoined him in the kitchen. "Some people might say you're wonderful for wanting to keep her things."

"Could be those people are right. But now it's time to let them go," he said with a sweep of his arm in the direction of the plates and cups on the table. "It's stupid thinking to cling too long to what is over."

Val reached for a sheet of tissue and began wrapping one of the teacups her grandmother had collected. She needed busywork desperately. Peripherally she saw her grandfather examining a potholder her grandmother had made. As he set it back in a kitchen drawer, Val wondered how her grandparents had managed to keep love alive, to weather some dark and disappointing moments and not lose that love.

"You're kind of quiet." Over his glasses, he peered at her. "You'll have a lot of people cheering you and Lucas on today."

"I know." Val offered a semblance of a smile before she left the kitchen for the garage to retrieve more cartons.

Expecting him to still be in the kitchen, she peeked into the living room to see if he'd joined the twins. Alone, they were somersaulting across his carpet.

"I'm in here," he said from the adjacent bedroom. "Got some things in here to get rid of, too."

She gave another look back at Brooke who had fixed her stare on a bud vase in the hutch. Before joining him, Val got the girls interested in their coloring books. For the next half hour, Val worked beside her grandfather and packed up clothes.

Lovingly he touched a brilliant blue sweater that had belonged to his wife. "Her eyes always looked so pretty when she wore this."

In silence, Val waited until he handed it to her, then she folded it. "Did we pack all of the clothes you wanted to get rid of?"

With a visual sweep of the bedroom, he nodded. "Yep."

Val folded flaps in on a carton and slid it to a corner of the bedroom.

"You take your grandmother's music box. The church doesn't need that. And she'd have wanted you to have it. You always played it when you came to visit."

The melody had soothed so many disturbing thoughts in her teenage mind back then. Her mother had been off with a new man. Somehow, she always seemed to find one during Val's summer vacation. By the time Val turned fifteen, she'd no longer believed her mother when she promised she'd be with her. Val had expected to spend the summer with her grandparents, had looked forward to the time with them.

"Let's finish in the kitchen."

Knowing better than to leave the twins alone too long, she nodded agreeably and followed him. "Besides the clothes and teacups, what are you giving to the church?"

"Your grandmother never liked those tablecloths in that drawer over there. She only kept them because her sister had given them, and she was too softhearted to dump them. I'm not."

Because he kept staring at her too closely, Val laughed softly. "I'll finish wrapping the teacups."

"Fine. I'll clean out the drawers. I guess I should have done this years ago. And not that I like admitting this, but I don't go for change too much."

Val grinned up at him and accepted the cup he'd already wrapped.

"You know I almost didn't ask Myrna out. Then I thought, What am I doing? Here's a lovely lady I enjoy talking to, so why am I acting like an idiot? I wanted to go out with her. She's smart. Interesting, too. I think she's read nearly every dang book in that library of hers. I like listening to her talk. Do you know what I mean?"

Val knew only too well. How often had she curled against Luke at night and felt a warm contentment just because he was near? When he'd talked to her then, he'd always done it in whispered tones, the private kind meant only for her, even though no one else had been in the house but them. To Val, those moments emphasized an intimacy that far exceeded passion.

"When your grandmother died, it hurt."

Val stilled while he puttered behind her in the kitchen. He'd never said those words to her before.

"I felt like someone had taken a piece of me away. She was all I ever wanted. Love at first sight," he said, looking up at Val. He blinked, but a shine remained in his eyes. "But it's time to start over. Can't do that, can you, if you don't let go of the past? People say I'm a stubborn old coot. Guess they're right. It took me a long time. It's hard to let go of the memories, good and bad, of someone you loved."

"Why would you want to?" Val asked, knowing she'd never forget Kelly. To forget would mean that Kelly had never existed.

"Well, you keep those memories," he clarified. "What you don't do is let them stop you from living. In a way, I'd been doing that until I met Myrna."

She smiled with him. "I'm glad you met her."

"Me, too." He beamed. "I think she might be exactly the type of woman I'd like to spend more time with."

So this is why he'd really asked her over, Val mused. "Are you asking for my approval?"

"I'm seventy-one. I don't need your approval," he said in a gruff tone that didn't faze Val. "But you do like her, don't you?"

"Very much, Gramps."

"That's what I'd hoped." His attempt to mask a pleased smile failed.

Before leaving his house, Val had glanced at the clock. She still had too much time left to think. Idleness promising to unnerve her, she rounded up the twins with a suggestion. "Why don't we go to the park?"

They both jumped up with glee.

"Polly, too?" Traci asked, strangleholding her doll.

"Of course, Polly, too."

For the next hour Val forgot everything but the joy on their faces as she pushed them on the swings. As mischievous as usual, they found the one puddle of mud left from the park's weekly irrigating.

Mud dripped from Traci's nose. Giggling, she grabbed a handful and tossed it.

Brooke shot a hesitant look at Val. With her nod, the little one plunged forward into the mud.

It had been a great way to spend an hour, Val decided when she and the twins entered the house later.

Slouched at a kitchen chair and reading the newspaper, when the back door opened, Luke raised his head and gaped at them. "Making mud pies today?"

Brooke wagged her head. "Threw mud. Vali, too." Tiny teeth flashed at him before they smiled up at Val.

"Sorry I missed all the fun," he said, reaching up and touching a dab of dried dirt near Val's eyebrow.

"It felt terrific," she admitted on a laugh before scooting the girls upstairs for baths.

Not until she and Luke stepped into the courtroom that afternoon did Val allow herself to think about what they would face at the hearing. It amazed her that an issue based on caring and loving should be decided on in a room that looked so cold and formal. "I'm not going to get emotional," she promised Luke when they sat at the table Harry's assistant had indicated.

Luke squeezed her hand. Hell, could anyone blame her if she did?

Dressed in a staid blue suit and prim white blouse, Charlene wiggled into her chair beside her lawyer, Kenneth Emerson.

Val noted that Charlene's husband hadn't joined them. How terrible it would be if she won, Val mused. Charlene only wanted the money and not the girls, and her husband wasn't even interested enough to appear for the court hearing.

"We've got a problem," Harry whispered as he joined her and Luke.

That wasn't what Val wanted to hear. "What problem?" she asked, and placed a hand to her stomach as it fluttered.

"Charlene's lawyer added a witness to their list."

With Val's shoulder against his upper arm, Luke was aware of her breaths quickening. He caught her hand. "Who, Harry?"

Harry tapped his arm to silence him as the judge appeared.

As Harry had predicted, Charlene's lawyer questioned Val about her job and about Kelly, then drilled Luke about his profession.

Val vaguely listened to Harry's rebuttal about Luke's dedication to medicine, and how he'd campaigned for better cardiac facilities at New Hope General. Few people knew that his efforts had been generated by a promise he'd made to himself after his father's death.

While each character witness for her and Luke and for their marriage was challenged, Val fretted about the twins. She tried to remember if she had told Myrna to give Traci her doll. Val thought so. And would Myrna remember to make them a midafternoon snack? Without one, Brooke would be ornery.

Bringing her attention back to the proceedings, Val saw that Irene was answering Harry's questions. "They have one of the strongest marriages I've ever seen," Irene said firmly. "Any couple who faces tragedy as they have and survives knows what marriage really means. They've stayed together despite their tragedy. That's a miracle."

Val drew a few more relaxing breaths as the woman who did their home study took the stand. When she finished, Val glanced at Luke. He met her with a dark, guarded stare, but the hand that closed over hers delivered a message that spoke volumes. Val, too, thought the woman's testimony had helped their case.

Then Charlene had her say. "I can't imagine them living with anyone but their Auntie Charlene." Tears flowed with perfect timing. "My dear cousin knew I was the best one to raise them, but the Kincaids were always over at Joe and Carrie's house, pretending to care for those sweet little girls, especially after they lost their own baby."

Though they'd answered questions by Charlene's lawyer about Kelly, Luke viewed her mention of Kelly as fighting dirty. "Stop this," he whispered to Harry, unsure how much Val could deal with.

Harry rose immediately. "Your Honor, this is incredible. Mrs. Kincaid has already testified that she and her husband have discussed having another child, that they don't view the Dawson twins as a substitute."

Charlene's lawyer popped to his feet. "Regardless of what they say, no one knows what they feel. There is a possibility that they do feel that way, especially Mrs. Kincaid. What other reason would she have for staying with her husband when their marriage is failing?"

Pure panic rippled through Val. How could he know that she and Luke had had trouble? How could he prove that? He couldn't, she quickly assured herself, unless—unless her grandfather or Jenny was called to testify. Val glanced back at both of them questioningly. In a discreet, subtle move, her grandfather shook his head. Jenny placed a hand over her mouth, sending a message that she wasn't the lawyer's source.

"How stable can a marriage be when the husband doesn't sleep in his bed?" Charlene's lawyer insisted after his client left the stand.

Val's mind raced with questions. If he hadn't talked to Jenny or her grandfather, then who was his witness? Who knew about Luke sleeping at the office? With the soft murmurings coming from the spectators behind her, Val turned a look over her shoulder. A heavy-set, unshaven man she'd never seen before entered the room.

"Damn," she heard Luke mutter.

"Who is that?" Val whispered.

"Arnie, one of the office cleaning crew," he whispered.

The knot in her stomach tightened.

Though Arnie Coleman shot a sheepish glance at Luke, he seemed aware of his own importance suddenly while being sworn in. "Sure did see him sleeping in his office," he answered in response to the question Charlene's lawyer asked. "Woke him up. I was there doing my job, dumping wastebaskets, cleaning bathrooms. When I went into his office, I saw him sleeping."

"When was this?"

"Days ago."

"Days ago," Charlene's lawyer emphasized, then turned an appealing look on the judge. "There is no marriage."

Voices buzzed through the courtroom. Val saw Jenny's ghost of an encouraging smile, Irene's distressed look, and her grandfather scowling in Charlene's direction.

"It's a meaningless union, Your Honor. And the Dawsons specifically stated that guardianship would go to the Kincaids only if their marriage was a solid and happy one. That hardly appears true."

Chapter Thirteen

Harry bolted from his chair to object.

Val didn't listen. They were going to lose. No one cared that the girls needed them.

"Val, come on."

She snapped a look at Luke. "What?" she asked, darting a glance at the judge. He was already stepping into his chambers. "What's happened?"

"A short recess."

"But we didn't get a chance to explain," she said, feeling almost panicky.

"Can you?" Harry asked quietly, leaning to see Luke on the other side of her.

"I can explain," he said, sounding far more confident than she felt.

How would he? Val wondered. He had been sleeping in the office during those weeks before they'd finally decided to divorce. The pressure of Luke's hand on her arm made her stand. With an agreement to meet Harry across the street at the diner, they left the courtroom.

Food was the last thing on her mind.

Inside the diner, as if sensing their need for privacy, even regulars who they knew, did nothing more than nod a hello. Val refused anything except coffee.

They were almost done with their coffee when Harry strolled in.

Unconsciously Val inched to the edge of her chair. "Arnie Coleman's testimony hurt us, didn't it?"

He cast a worried look at Luke before answering her. "Okay, Valerie. I'm not going to pretend nothing will go wrong. We all know it's possible. Charlene is a blood relative, and questions have been raised about that one stipulation in the Dawsons' last will and testament."

"So reputations and character references be damned," Luke said, unable to quell the irritation intensifying within him.

Harry waited while the waitress took his order for coffee. "You said you could explain. Just tell me why you were there."

"I had emergency room duty until midnight, but a long-time patient of mine, John Rontering called at the hospital, concerned because his four-year-old granddaughter had pains on the right side. I told him to bring her to the hospital, and stayed there until he did." He paused while Harry's coffee was set in front of him. "After I performed an emergency appendectomy, it was three-thirty in the morning. I was tired.

Too tired to drive. So I went to my office for a couple of hours' sleep.''

Harry still looked concerned. "I guess that makes sense. Doctors do stay late with patients, and when exhausted might find the closest place to sleep. But this will all depend on how the judge interpreted Arnie Coleman's testimony.''

Val had learned the danger in clinging to false hopes.

Nearly an hour and a half passed before they returned to the courthouse.

Maybe it was because he'd been helpless to save his own child that Luke felt so desperate to give the twins the love and stability they needed, to make sure the twins stayed with a woman who'd be as caring as their own mother. "We won't lose them," he said softly to Val. "We'll fight for them. If this doesn't go our way, we'll fight. Believe me. Everything will be all right.''

More than doubt clouded her eyes. He saw an anguish that made him ache, the same look that had been in her eyes the night after they'd lost their child.

"Come on," Harry urged, rushing to them as they reached the courthouse steps.

Val moved mechanically between Luke and Harry. She felt outside of herself, as if she were watching them cross the highly polished floor to the courtroom. She knew she returned Jenny's smile. She knew she squeezed Irene's hand for a second, but she felt detached from herself. Sitting on the chair at the table they'd been at before, she clutched her hands in her lap. Seconds ticked by like an eternity before the judge entered.

Everyone quieted when Harry urged Luke with a nod of his head to explain.

"I have only one more question," Harry said after Luke told about the emergency that night. "Do you love your wife?"

It was a question Luke hadn't expected, but not one that he had any difficulty answering. "There's never been a moment since I married her when I didn't love her."

The softness in Val's eyes told him that she understood what he was trying to say. Not even when they weren't talking, when they'd been on the verge of divorce, had he stopped loving her.

"I'll make a decision shortly," the judge said.

Val watched him leave the courtroom. She heard the soft buzz of conversation behind her, but felt too frozen to the spot to even turn her head. Clutching her hands together, she saw Harry's assistant rush up, but couldn't hear what she said.

After she left, Harry offered a strange comment. "You may have chosen the perfect career, Lucas."

Stone-faced, the judge reappeared. Val thought he could have bluffed his way to winning any poker game.

"Before making a ruling, certain issues had to be considered. The court does prefer to place a child with blood relatives."

Charlene sat taller, beaming.

Val gripped Luke's hand tightly.

"I realize emotions have to be considered, but equally important is the welfare of the children," the judge went on. "The court must determine who would provide the best home for a child while considering the laws of the state.''

Words muffled. All Val could hear was the pounding of her own heart. *Please, God, let us keep them. We love them.*

He was saying something now about Joe and Carrie's wishes having been public knowledge. "At that time, Mrs. Evans should have challenged such an agreement. Since she didn't, I have reached the conclusions that she had ample time to contest her cousin and his wife's guardianship plans.'' His gaze moved from Charlene to them. ''The court-appointed representative has found the Kincaids' marriage, as required in the custodial agreement, to be sound and stable. As for questions regarding that, I have a son who also chose medicine as a career. Doctors' hours are often erratic and exhausting.'' Unexpectedly a slip of a smile edged his lips. ''Therefore, I must honor Joseph and Carolyn Dawson's wishes. My decision must favor Dr. and Mrs. Kincaid.''

Luke felt Val sag against him with relief.

''This hearing is concluded. You are free to leave.''

''We should thank the judge's son,'' Harry said, amused.

For the first time since they'd left home, Val honestly felt like smiling. Across the aisle, she saw Charlene's lawyer shrug his shoulders. On a huff, Charlene bound to her feet and stormed from the room. All Val wanted at that moment was to wrap her arms around Brooke and Traci.

At the door of the courtroom, she paused for barely a second, watching Charlene's clipped pace past the twins, who had just arrived with Myrna. Val rushed to where the three of them stood with Luke's mother. As she squatted down, little arms curled around her neck. Her heart drumming, she held them tightly and drew in a breath, wondering if anything smelled as sweet as they did.

"Of course, they won," her grandfather was saying to Myrna and others who gathered around.

Val squeezed the girls to her and looked up at Luke. She believed they had won in more ways than anyone might know. Pushing to a stand, she laced her fingers with his.

"We have to celebrate," Irene insisted. "A cake is waiting, and so are friends."

"You planned a party?" Val asked, amazed at Irene's positive thinking.

"Yes, I did. How could they not find in your favor?"

Irene's home filled with conversation and laughter. For the next few hours the party grew with more well-wishers drifting into the house to offer congratulations.

Exhausted but happy, Val laughed at her grandfather's unrestrained comments. "I thought I'd puke when Charlene started bawling and sniffling. She should have gone into acting."

"I never doubted the outcome," Neil assured Luke, patting him on the back.

Val wished she had felt so certain, but she'd been racked with fear.

"It's been a terribly long day," Irene said, suddenly beside Val. She scanned the table bearing cups, plates and forks. "I see my sheet cake is a big hit. I have another one in the kitchen." She looked at Val then. "We also need some more cookies. Would you help me?"

"Of course." Val followed her, and took over the task of placing more cookies on one of Irene's crystal serving plates.

"I can't tell you how pleased I am, Valerie. I'd hoped that when you and Lucas decided to battle Charlene for the twins that meant you were truly together again."

Val raised her head slowly to meet her mother-in-law's eyes and saw Luke standing in the doorway.

Astonishment edged his voice. "You knew that we—"

His mother swung a gentle smile on him. "Did you think I wouldn't notice?" Her attention went back to Val. "I was there when Kelly died. I saw the two of you. The world shattered for both of you that night." Looking down, she sliced a fancy decorated chocolate cake. "But I kept hoping you'd work out your problems."

Luke read the unspoken question in Val's eyes. How many other people had they thought they'd fooled who'd guessed that they weren't the town's most perfect married couple?

"I'll take the cake into the other room. Will you bring the cookies, Valerie?" she asked, and touched Luke's arm in passing.

Val wondered if she was gaping. "Yes, I'll bring them."

A grin curved a corner of Luke's mouth. "Guess I'd better not quit my day job and try acting."

An easy smile sprang to Val's lips. "Me, either." She rounded the table and stepped into Luke's arms.

"Enjoying yourself?" he asked against her lips.

"More now," she murmured. Tenderly his hand coursed down her arm. It was with the kind of ease that conveyed a deeper intimacy than simply sex. Val pressed her cheek against his. "I plan to later, too," she whispered in his ear.

It was nearly dusk when Luke unlocked their door. Like her, he seemed to want to linger over the girls. Taking their time, they read stories before tucking the girls in for a quick nap before dinner.

Reality still hadn't settled over her, Val realized. She felt as if she needed a pinch to make sure she wasn't dreaming. They had won the right to raise the twins as their own. She and Luke were their parents now. "I feel wonderful," she said softly as she glanced back from the bedroom doorway at the sleeping girls. "I guess I was afraid to believe."

Luke caught her at the waist as they descended the steps. So much time had passed since he'd seen her face glowing with such happiness. "I told you everything would be all right."

"Yes, I know," she said distractedly, spotting a toy on a step. "But you said the same thing before, about Kelly and—" Bent over, picking up the toy block, she realized what she'd just done. She wished for the moment back. Why had she even mentioned that night? She wanted them to be happy, to celebrate, to love. She wanted nothing to spoil the joy they'd been feeling. Too late, she realized, tilting a look up at him. There was no smile in his eyes anymore.

Letting her go, he stepped back. What he'd dreaded most was upon them again. Foolishly he'd convinced himself this moment wouldn't happen, but in the back of his mind, he'd always known a dark, heavy cloud of despair hung over them, waiting for the first opportunity to burst, to wash away everything they'd found. "I'll finish it. She died, even though I told you everything would be all right," he said quietly, longing for his own deafness at that second so he couldn't hear his words.

And nothing had made any sense, Val reflected. Even breathing and eating and sleeping had taken enormous effort.

He wanted to pull her close, make love with her so his mind went blank to everything but her in his arms. He knew he'd already lost the chance. "I need to call my service," he said, moving away from her.

Val saw the rigid set of his features. He was distancing himself from her again. "Luke, you must have had doubts, too."

More than his share, he realized as one painful memory loomed over them. No matter how much love existed, shadows chased them of that time when they'd been useless to each other, when pain had been the only emotion. "You can't forget, can you?"

When he faced her, she felt as if he were looking straight through her. She was misinterpreting what he was saying. She had to be. "Forget Kelly? Do you expect me to ever forget our daughter?"

No, never her. Whether she realized it or not, that wasn't what she couldn't forget. Though he'd started for the den, he crossed to the screen door and stared out at the night sky.

Despite feeling a little dazed, Val was thinking clearly enough to know that silence now would eventually destroy them, just as it nearly had before. "Will you please talk to me?"

He faced her slowly, what-ifs plaguing him. "Tell me something. What if we hadn't won?"

She felt cold and alone again. "We did."

"Answer me. What if we hadn't?"

"Why are you doing this?"

Why was he? Maybe because he knew he couldn't live anymore with what she'd never admitted.

Val let out a soft breath. "I don't know what you want me to say. We did win. I prayed for that. I wanted to believe we would."

"But you didn't believe me, did you?"

"It's not so simple."

An ache for both of them skittered through him. The unspoken blame still lingered. She'd never said the words. She would deny feeling that way, but he would never forget the anguish in her eyes when he'd promised her Kelly would be all right, or the accusations after she'd died. "I didn't know what to do that night for you—or her." They stood no more than inches from each other and he couldn't touch her. "I'm a doctor," he said fiercely, angrily. "I'm dedicated to saving people, and I was helpless to do anything for our own child."

Torment darkened his eyes. Val caught a breath, feeling as if someone had punched her hard in the stomach. "You blamed yourself?" she asked, nearly choking on the words.

Pain twisted in his gut. "And you blamed me."

Nothing prepared her for those words. Stunned, she needed a second to let them register. "That's not true." She shook her head wildly with denial. "I never—"

Angrily he cut her off. "Dammit, don't!" He was hurting so badly that he felt as if something had tightened its fist inside him and was squeezing hard. "Don't lie to yourself anymore."

Myriad emotions jumbling inside her, Val took a step back from him. "I don't know what I felt," she finally admitted with his eyes challenging her to face that awful night again. Self-defensively she seized anger because he was backing her into a corner. "I was hurting," she said, trying to explain.

"So was I."

His words rang in her ears. Struggling to breathe evenly, she whirled away as feelings rushed forward that she'd thought she'd buried on a cool February day at the cemetery.

Behind her, she heard the squeaking of the door opening. She knew even before it slammed shut that she was alone. She didn't move. She couldn't. Tears streaming down her cheeks, she swayed back against the kitchen counter. *Oh, God, she had blamed him.*

Chapter Fourteen

Luke needed to be alone, needed time to bury the anger threatening to explode. No, it wasn't anger. Guilt shadowed him. It had since that night.

He ambled to his car, drawing in breaths like a man fighting for each one after nearly drowning. He felt a stickiness on the air that announced a storm was rolling in. He wished for the sound of rain to end the stillness around him, to help him dodge his own thoughts.

Stupidly he thought he had freed himself of the memories that had occurred like nightmares even when he'd been awake. But they swirled around in his mind now.

The sense of helplessness for his child fighting to stay alive, for his wife alone when the doctors had whisked her tiny daughter from her because she was laboring to breathe.

The subtle change in Val as she retreated from him as if only she understood her pain. He had wanted to yell at her back then. *Hey, I'm hurting, too.* He'd never said those words until minutes ago. He'd kept his scar covered, concealing it from prying eyes. But even today, it still festered.

He stared at the dark silhouettes of trees and remembered now the shocked look on Val's face when he suggested they consider having another baby, as if he were committing some betrayal to Kelly's memory. He could even hear the sound of her voice, so gentle, as if apologizing, when she said no.

He remembered, too, the quiet resignation that had slipped over him when they discussed divorce.

Softly he cursed. There was nothing more to say now. And he had no idea where he was going. He'd only known that he needed to get out of the house.

Inside his car, he flicked on the ignition, then pulled away from the curb. With no destination in mind, he drove toward the edge of town. It occurred to him that he and Val had nearly made it. They really had. He'd felt love when he held her in his arms. All the magic had returned just as understanding had stretched between them during unexpected moments. Laughter had filled the house again. He could have pretended. No, he couldn't.

And he couldn't fight this, not anymore. No matter how much he wanted to believe differently, they had no chance. Despite so much seeming right between them, he'd known she hadn't really forgotten or forgiven him.

Looking up, he saw a red light at the last minute and slammed his foot on the brake pedal. He glanced around him. Where the hell was he going? He'd driven to the edge of New Hope.

The light changed to green, but he didn't hit the accelerator. He sat, staring ahead of him at the darkness beyond the town's streetlights. Nothing existed beyond this point.

On a hard breath, he swayed back against the seat and rubbed his hand over his face. He'd find nothing without her. Nothing.

Val clung to the edge of the kitchen counter. Closing her eyes didn't help, didn't banish the look she'd seen in Luke's eyes.

A queasiness grabbing hold, she took several deep breaths to block the sensation. She'd always thought if they loved each other, they could deal with anything. But they hadn't been able to.

That was her fault.

Deep down, she had been blaming him. She'd been weary from the emotional roller coaster that had come after their child's birth. When he'd come to her in the recovery room, she'd nearly shrieked at him to do something. It had been ridiculous to say that. And unreasonable. But it had seemed so cruel to her that he could save others and couldn't save their daughter. When he'd promised her Kelly would be all right, she'd clung to those words. She knew now they'd been uttered by a man hurting as much as her, seizing hope like a lifeline.

On that night, though, she'd been aware of nothing but her own torment. When Kelly had died, she hadn't been able to rid her mind of one thought. He'd broken a promise to her about their daughter. Desperately she'd needed someone—anyone—to blame, and he had been so accessible.

Sounds drifted down the stairs, indicating the twins had awakened. Slowly Val climbed to the second floor. It hadn't been coldness she'd seen in Luke's eyes all those months. He'd pulled into himself to hide his hurt—hurt she'd caused.

With the tips of her fingers, she blotted the tears at the corners of her eyes and on her cheeks. She stopped in the bathroom and splashed water on her face. For the twins' sake, somehow she'd veil the turmoil inside her. Don't think. Don't feel, she told herself. Not now. Whatever was happening between her and Luke wasn't going away, but she had to concentrate on the twins.

Full of energy for some reason, they scrambled down the steps. Val braced herself emotionally and settled in the living room with them. Repeatedly she glanced at the clock. When would he come back? What if he didn't this time?

Expecting the girls to start yelling for dinner, she pushed herself from the sofa and strolled into the kitchen. A hand on the refrigerator door, she was certain she heard Luke's car pulling onto the driveway. She swung around and rushed toward the window.

She never reached it.

Her right foot came down crookedly on something. Like a tightrope walker, she threw her arms out to keep her balance, but her legs went out from under her. Her buttocks hit the floor hard, jarring her, rearing back her head. As the side of it slammed against the stove, pain shot through her skull.

Moaning, Val blinked against the flash of light and a second of light-headedness. Eyes squeezed shut, she lifted a hand, wincing when her fingers touched the spot above her temple. For a long moment she dealt with the initial pain. As it gave way to a persistent throbbing, she opened her eyes. To her right, she spotted the culprit that had caused her fall—a miniature plastic car.

It was then, too, that she saw Traci standing in the doorway, staring at her. Before Val could say anything to her, she burst into tears.

"Shh, come here." Val opened her arms to her. "Come here," she urged.

Tears streaming down her cheeks, Traci scrambled onto her lap. Val cuddled her, smoothing back her bangs and kissing her forehead. "Don't cry." She raised her head slowly and saw Brooke, wide-eyed, feet from them.

"Vali okay?" The panic in her voice was unmistakable.

"Yes." Uncertain how steady she'd be if she stood, Val stayed still and offered her other hand to Brooke.

Her small body trembled as she nuzzled into Val. "Mama go 'way." With her face buried in Val's shoulder, she shook her head. "Vali no go 'way?" she cried.

Val's heart squeezed. Though Traci had shown some anxiety since Joe and Carrie's death, Brooke had seemed to acccpt the absence of her parents the best. Val sensed now that she'd simply repressed heartache and tucked it into a private place within her. Like Luke had? she wondered.

For the little girl in her arms, Val chose the only words she knew to help. "I won't go away." Pulling back, she met the eyes glistening with tears. If only she could assure her that she wouldn't lose everyone she loved, but... Oh, God. Val brought both girls tightly to her. How could she? she wondered. How could she explain that to a two-year-old when she hadn't understood that herself for too long?

You can't make a new start if you don't let go of the past, her grandfather had said. Had she done that? She thought she'd gone on with her life. She'd stopped crying whenever she thought about Kelly, and she'd found that she still had plenty of love left in her to give to the twins. But when Luke had wanted to have another baby, she'd refused.

Why seemed suddenly so clear. The past had clouded her present and her future. But at what point had she become so afraid of the risk to her heart? With Kelly's death? Or as a child herself? she wondered, remembering the disappointment and heartache she'd felt when her mother's promises had been broken. There had been so many of them. And how often had she thought one of her mother's husbands would be a father to her? The father she never had, never even knew.

Looking down at the twins' blond heads, Val swallowed hard against the knot in her throat. Until this moment, until she'd seen herself through two little girls, she hadn't even been aware of the pain she'd been harboring. Or of the fear.

Briefly she must have eluded it when she married Luke, but it had reared its ugly head when she lost Kelly. It had reminded her how easy it was to love and lose.

Oh, Luke, what have I done to us?

In his eyes, she'd read his suffering and his grief. It had been no less than hers, but she'd forgotten about him. She'd only thought about her own anguish. And because she'd been so afraid of losing, she'd kept herself from taking the final step with him that would bind them again—becoming a family.

"Vali," Brooke cried.

Swallowing hard, she pressed her lips together in a semblance of a smile, too aware of the twins' frightened stares. "I'm okay, honey." She soothed Brooke and hugged her and Traci tightly.

He wasn't sure why he returned home. Mostly he wasn't sure she'd be there. Luke pulled in the driveway behind her car. It hadn't been moved. Switching off the ignition, he stared at the house bright with lights now. Though he stepped from the car, he stood for a long moment beside it. He didn't know what to say to her anymore, he realized. Or had it all been said?

Uncertainty accompanied the ache inside him as he strolled to the door. No coward, he didn't hesitate at opening the back door.

Instantly his heart lurched. On the floor, braced against the stove, Val held what looked like a bloody cloth to her head. Like bookends, the twins nestled against her. Shouting her name, he crossed the kitchen in three strides. "What happened?"

"I fell and hit my head," she answered, setting the twins on their feet beside her.

As she made a move, he nearly swore. "Stay still." His heart pounding hard against his chest, he gently lifted the wet, sticky cloth from her head.

"I didn't want to get up for ice," she tried to explain while she dealt with the throbbing from even a slight movement. "So I dipped a dishtowel in Brooke's cold fruit punch."

The panic rising within Luke receded. No blood. Fruit punch. With a doctor's eye, he examined the bump.

"I'm okay."

"Like hell you are."

A matching set of blue eyes stared up at him and widened.

"Luke," Val said through barely moving lips, "don't frighten them."

What about me? he nearly yelled. "You're going to the hospital."

"I don't need to. I'm really..." Val gave up arguing as he gathered her in his arms.

He wanted to sit there with her for a moment and hold her, tell her that he was sorry for everything. He fought his own need and carried her to the car.

After he settled her into the passenger's seat, he fastened the twins in their car seats. Using the cellular phone, he made a call to the hospital the moment he backed out of the driveway.

Hundreds of times during the past months, Luke had walked down the hospital corridor past the waiting room. Whenever he'd been seeing patients or been there for surgery, he'd somehow divorced himself from the memory of the last time he'd sat on the waiting room sofa. With a clearness that pained him, he recalled that February night. The run from ER after learning that his newborn daughter was dying, sitting with Val in the recovery room. Feeling impatient and powerless, he'd finally left her and sought the pediatrician and the heart specialist in charge. Colleagues of his, they'd merely shaken their heads when he found them.

Numb, he'd started back to the recovery room, but had seen his mother and Edwin on that sofa and told them about their granddaughter's death. He'd felt drained—empty. And the walk to the recovery room, and Val, had seemed endless. Nothing had ever prepared him for the anguish he felt when he delivered the news to his wife that their daughter had died.

Nothing, he realized, and looked down as he felt movement beside him. Snuggling closer to him, Traci raised a face marred by too much worry for someone so young. Luke gripped her tighter. On the other side of him, Brooke slouched against the sofa cushion with her head bowed. Her quietness frightened him. The only time he'd seen a child so still, the boy had been terribly sick.

He said her name softly. "Brooke?"

As she slowly raised her head, he saw the tears streaking her chubby cheeks and opened his arm to her, praying she would let him hold her.

She fell against him, her tiny arm draping across his midsection. "'Fraid." She whimpered and shook her head. "Vali say no go 'way."

Luke lowered his head. "What?"

"Vali say so."

It didn't take much to guess the conversation that had existed between the girls and Val before he arrived home. With her eyes on him, he searched for the right words now to comfort her. "She's not going anywhere." He tightened his embrace, realizing in such a short time how much he'd come to love both of the girls.

"Lu-cas go?"

Lightly he stroked her hair. He knew he couldn't guarantee that he would be there when they woke up in the morning or when they wanted a book read at night. But he'd made a commitment he planned to keep. He'd always be near for them. "No, I'm not going away, either."

Curling against him, she popped her thumb into her mouth.

He waited for her eyes to meet his again. "Cross my heart," he said, and gave her a smile.

Her serious, blue eyes searched his face for an uncomfortably long moment. "'Kay."

Within minutes, he knew by her deep even breaths that she, too, like Traci, had fallen asleep.

Nearby the elevator doors opened. "Lucas." His mother rushed toward him. In her haste to come to the hospital, she'd slipped on two different shoes. A step behind her, Val's grandfather wore the same grim look he had the night of Kelly's birth.

Luke whispered an assurance to both of them. "She's in X ray now."

"She bumped her head?" Edwin asked quietly. "How?"

"I don't know, but except for a mild concussion, she seemed okay to me."

"Oh." His mother heaved a sigh.

"If you'd sit with the twins, I'll go see what's happening."

His mother was already on the other side of Traci and easing her from the crook of his arm.

"I'll hold Brooke," Edwin said, and worked his way into the vacated spot.

Luke had meant what he said about Val to his mother and Edwin. Still, the need to see her overwhelmed him.

* * *

Resting her head back on the pillow, Val closed her eyes and felt herself inching toward a foul mood. She hated the dumb hospital gown. She hated being in the hospital. Everyone had asked the same question. Does your head hurt? It seemed like a silly question to her. Of course, it hurt. But she wanted to go home. She needed to be with the girls. She needed to talk to Luke.

What if it was too late? What words would soften the hurt? Even as her head throbbed, she wiggled to the edge of the mattress to dangle her feet.

"What are you doing?"

Wincing, she gripped the sheet, not the least bit fazed by Luke's authoritative doctor tone. "I'm going home."

He eyed the red lump at the edge of her hairline. "Guess again."

"I don't want to stay here."

He realized it had been a long time since he'd seen her stubborn streak. "Too bad." He walked to the chart hanging at the end of the bed. His colleague's scribble was worse than his, but Luke deciphered enough to feel relief sweep through him.

"Is that your best bedside manner?"

"My best," he confirmed.

He sounded angry to her. "It's a miracle you have any patients." Val frowned at the crown of his head. "What does it say?"

"That you need to be watched." For another moment he kept his eyes on the chart. He'd been damn scared when he'd seen her on the floor with that cloth against her head. "You have to stay tonight."

Annoyed at her predicament and exasperated with him at the moment, she heaved a sigh. "I'd like to see the twins. Do doctors have some special privileges?"

He'd give her whatever she wanted. "If there's trouble getting them in here, I'll sneak them in to see you."

Val's mood gentled. Of course he would. He'd always done his best for her. Always. "We need to talk, don't we?" she asked softly. All that had passed between them during those painful moments couldn't be ignored. He'd realized first what had slowly dawned on her. They'd never heal what was wrong with their marriage until they shared honest feelings about Kelly's death.

Val took a hard breath and stared down at her hands, at the engagement ring she'd loved from the moment he'd placed it on her finger, at the wedding band that had symbolized how much they loved each other.

From outside the room, two nurses chattered while passing by, their rubber soles squeaking with each step they took. "You should rest," Luke said.

Val gave her head a shake and winced again. "No, don't do that," she appealed as he started for the door. "We have to face this."

Under his breath, he cursed. He wanted to avoid this now. Almost desperately he wanted to tell her to lay down, and he wanted to get out of the room before more words that could only hurt both of them were said.

"Luke, we can't run from it."

Run. That's exactly what he wanted to do. But he'd done that once already. Nothing has changed, he realized. He told himself that he would prove she could depend on him, but he was ready to flee, like before, and escape into silence to avoid more painfully honest moments. No, he couldn't run anymore.

As he shut the door for privacy, Val prodded herself to say what he needed to hear. "Unfairly, I faulted you for not doing the impossible—saving our daughter," she said softly. Her heart twisted with the admittance. While she'd protected herself from more pain, she'd hurt him badly. "How could you be to blame for anything that happened? Nothing was your fault."

Her words didn't soothe him. "Be honest, Val," he said on a hard breath. "Admit you can't forget that I let you down."

She realized she'd hit her head, but she wasn't confused until this second. "Let me down. How did you do that?"

"You have to ask?" he practically shouted. "Have you really forgotten that you were alone when you had Kelly?"

"Luke." She started to move from the bed.

He crossed to her in two strides. "What the hell are you doing?"

"I want you near."

"You're crazy," he said, cupping her shoulders and easing her back on the bed.

Val wouldn't lay down. "Where were you that night?" She didn't wait for his answer. "In surgery."

That didn't ease his conscience. His wife had been caught in a medical emergency of her own. To his mind, there was no acceptable excuse. When she'd been told their daughter might not live, she'd been alone. "I know I failed you and Kelly."

She understood now. "And if you can't accept that, why should I be able to?"

He ached being so near and not touching her. "That was my fault, Val. I should have been there for you."

How had she let so much go wrong between them? She loved him. You don't hurt the person you love. Val closed her eyes, but there was no way to block out what she'd done. Through silence and withdrawal after Kelly's death, she'd convinced him that more than grief had caused her to pull away from him. She'd made him believe that in her eyes he was guilty of not saving Kelly, of failing her as a doctor and father. And of letting his wife down.

Val pressed her lips together. What a burden he'd suffered with all this time. Looking up at him, she swallowed hard. This wasn't time for tears. "So now what?"

His eyes narrowed as if trying to see inside her.

"Do we forget all we've worked for? Do we let the twins down?"

"Dammit, you know I wouldn't do that."

"Yes, I do know that. I know the kind of man you are. You were there for your mother when she needed you. You did all you could for Kelly. And you've always been there for me." She clutched his hand, afraid he'd pull away. "All those months when I turned away from you, you never gave up on us until I forced you to when I said I wanted to move."

If she lost him, for the rest of her life, she'd be haunted by memories, more good than bad. And she wanted to make more memories with him. "You've never done anything wrong. I have," she admitted.

"Stop it!"

As he jerked back, she used the only leverage she had. "I swear if you take one step away, I'm out of this bed."

"Don't be dumb. You were hurt badly."

Val waited until he stepped closer again. "Yes, I was. And so were you because I kept us apart. I should have looked for another chance to have everything we'd once had, to have everything we possibly could have together," she said, tugging on his hand to make him sit beside her. "I'm sorry. I'm so sorry for what I've put you through, but I was so caught up in the loss that I kept pulling away, even when you wanted to have another baby." She held his hand tighter, afraid if she let go, he'd be gone.

Luke might have pulled back, but his mind cleared with her next words.

"I was afraid, afraid to lose again."

"To lose?"

Sadness for both of them heavy in her heart, Val nodded. A soft understanding came into the eyes on her. Later, she'd tell him feelings she'd had because of her childhood. Right now, he needed to hear other words. "I love you. I want to work this out. I need you," she whispered on a shuddery breath.

That was the last thing Luke had expected to hear her say to him.

His silence unnerved her. She couldn't believe she'd done so much damage. "Do you still love me?" she asked hesitantly.

It amazed him that she had any doubts. "You know I do." Leaning forward, she caressed his cheek. To have her touch again seemed like a miracle to him. Closing his eyes, he brought her hand to his lips. "I told the truth today. I've never not loved you."

Finally, Val mused. She tilted her head back so her eyes were level with his. "We are *not* going to throw everything away, are we? Two little girls need us—you and me. And—" She made a small sound as he slipped his arms around her. Relief and pleasure rose inside her. He held her with such strength, but there had been a time when he'd needed to lean on someone. If only she'd been there for him.

"And I need you," he murmured. He'd been dying inside at the thought of never feeling her in his arms or seeing her smile at him again.

Val pulled back, unable to stop tears as she stared into the gaze searching hers. "So we'll take a second chance?"

No more distance between them, Luke told himself, resting his forehead on hers. If he'd held her, he'd have crushed her to him. "Depends." Her fingers stilled on his face. "Want to marry me?"

Joy filling her, she gave in to a short laugh. "We are married," she reminded him, and framed his jaw with her hands.

"Again," he said, smiling now because, despite tears, she was. Behind him, he heard the click of the door opening, but with her mouth hovering close to his all he could think about was the taste of her. "I love you," he murmured against her lips.

"I..." Hearing squeals, Val sniffed and blotted away the moisture on her face before she looked over his shoulder toward the door.

As Brooke and Traci charged into the room, Luke backed off the bed. The moment he lifted the girls up to the bed, they pounced forward to reach Val. Little arms curled around her neck and hugged her hard.

Val laughed with happiness as Brooke tugged Luke's hand so he sat again and treated him to a kiss on the cheek. "I love you," Val finished when his gaze returned to her. Holding Traci, she swayed into him for the kiss she'd barely gotten before the invasion. "Guess this proves what everyone believes. We're all perfect for each other."

With her quick kiss, Luke let the moment seep over him and grinned at the three women in his life. Despite all the hurt, he'd learned something valuable. To keep love alive, he couldn't run from emotions ever again. Before a too serious mood slipped over him, he wiggled fingers that promised to tickle in the girls' direction.

The pleased audience of two giggled with delight.

Val hadn't thought it possible she'd ever love him more than she once had, but her heart swelled with emotion. "There's something else you should know," she said softly.

The smile in her eyes made him tighten his arm at her back. "What's that?"

Lovingly Val caressed his cheek. He needed to know once and for all that he'd never failed anyone, especially their daughter. "You're a wonderful daddy."

*   *   *   *   *

*Don't miss the next book
in Silhouette's exciting
DADDY KNOWS LAST series.*

Here's a sneak preview of

HOW TO HOOK A HUSBAND
(AND A BABY)

*by Carolyn Zane
available in October from
Silhouette Yours Truly*

How To Hook a Husband
(and a Baby)

—◄ ►—

"Bang, bang! You're dead!"

Blowing on his imaginary pistol, Dustin Donovan shrieked with glee and crawled behind the couch as fast as his five-year-old knees could carry him.

Wendy Wilcox, his baby-sitter, next door neighbor and dearest buddy affected her scariest voice. "Oh, no, I ain't, you biscuit-eating sidewinder," she shouted from behind the chair-and-blanket tent they'd built in the middle of her living room.

Reaching into the breast pocket of her postal uniform for a handkerchief, she thrust it through the tent opening and waved it at Dusty. "Hey, sagebrush breath," she called, and watched him drop back behind the couch, giggling all the while. "I want to make a treaty with you, you crazy, milk-mustached, cow puncher... and there's chocolate milk in it for you."

Silence.

Wendy grinned. She knew how much he loved chocolate milk. "And I just rustled up some peanut butter and jelly rations." Again, silence. "Plus, I got us some chocolate chip cookies . . ."

Dusty groaned. "Okay," he agreed and clumped across the floor to settle next to Wendy at her coffee table. "But, we're not done yet," he informed her.

Tossing Dustin a small package of cookies, Wendy reached for a pile of books and magazines she'd bought earlier that day. The blurb on the cover of the latest copy of *Metropolitan* magazine blared Do You Have What It Takes To Snare A Man? She shrugged. Obviously not, or she'd have done it by now.

Her gaze wandered to the book titles stacked in front of her. *I'm Okay... We're All Okay, So Why Am I Still Single?* One book wondered, *Are You Everybody's Friend, Nobody's Lover?* Yep, she answered. *How To Be Irresistible To Every Man, Every Time.* She didn't want to be irresistible to every man. Just one likable lug. She ran her fingers over her personal favorite, *How To Hook A Husband.* Hopefully, with all this advice she'd have that man in no time. Because, if the article she'd read last week held even a speck of truth, she had to do *something* if she was ever going to have a family of her own.

Women over thirty—it had gloomily prophesied—had little or no chance of ever tying the knot. And Wendy was only a month away from the big Three-Oh.

The Big Three-Oh-No.

Gadzooks! she thought, taking a big swig of her chocolate milk. She'd better get a move on. Time was running out.

Travis Donovan pulled to a stop in his driveway and cut the engine of his large, American-made, 4-wheel-drive pickup. Tonight, Travis wanted nothing more than to spend a few minutes wrestling with his five-year-old son, then off to dreamland.

His glance swept next door to Wendy's place and landed on her picture window. Several lamps illuminated his son and Wendy as they gamboled around her disheveled living room. Travis grinned. Thank God for good old Wendy. She was a good egg, that Wendy. Real salt of the earth.

Hunching thoughtfully over his steering wheel, Travis watched the two at play. Yep, she was nice enough, but personally, he couldn't see the dazzling attraction his son had for her. Squinting at Wendy, he figured that she was probably just about as different from the women he usually dated as two women could be. Yc-cs...definitely not for him. Though Travis knew that Dusty wanted him to fall madly in love with Wendy and make her his mommy.

Travis hopped out of his truck and bound across the yard. As he drew nearer, he could hear his son's giddy laughter and smiled to himself at the infectious sound. Peering through the darkness, he located the doorbell and alerted them to his arrival.

Flipping on the porch light, Wendy peeked through the peephole and then unlocked the dead bolt. Just as she'd suspected, it was Travis. A quick glance at the clock on the hall table told her that it was after midnight. Shaking her head, she pulled open the door and found him standing there, looking for all the world like Brad Pitt after a rough ride with Thelma and Louise.

"Come on in," she said, pushing her glasses up on her nose.

Travis dimpled as he caught his son midair and swung the noisy child up onto his back. Turning, Wendy led them to the living room where she began gathering up Dustin's belongings and stuffing them into his knapsack.

Travis lifted his cowboy hat off his son's head and slid it easily onto his own thick brown hair. He set Dusty on his feet, then stretched tiredly and joined Wendy on the couch. "Man, am I tired, or—" Travis stared intently at the coffee table in front of him. "What?" he asked distractedly.

Wendy felt her stomach sink. The books. Damn. She should have known better than to leave them out for all the world to see. But what difference did it make? It was no secret that she was pretty much of a flop in the ingenue department.

Lifting his eyes, Travis arched a skeptical brow and smirked. *"How To Hook A Husband?"* He chuckled and reached for the stack of books and magazines. "You're... hunting for a husband?" Hooting at the ceiling, he pushed his head back and let the laughter flow.

Reaching over, Wendy snatched her precious books from his arms and fought the urge to smack his gorgeous, perfect face. "I'd appreciate it if you'd stop laughing."

"Why?"

"Why what?" she snapped.

He snorted. "Why all the advice on how to land a man?"

"Because," she cried, "I'm going to be thirty!" She stared plaintively at him, as though this fact explained everything.

"So?" Travis shrugged, puzzled.

"So..." Wendy sighed, exasperated at the obtuse male mind. *So, no more Mrs. Nice Guy,* she thought. Setting her jaw with determination, she glared at Travis. "So, I'm going to be engaged by my thirtieth birthday," she announced grimly, "or know the reason why."

* * * * *

There's nothing quite like a family

REUNION

HANNAH MICHAEL KATE

The new miniseries by
Pat Warren

Three siblings are about to be reunited.
And each finds love along the way....

HANNAH
Her life is about to change now that she's met
the irresistible Joel Merrick in HOME FOR HANNAH
(Special Edition #1048, August 1996).

MICHAEL
He's been on his own all his life. Now he's
going to take a risk on love...and
take part in the reunion he's been
waiting for in MICHAEL'S HOUSE
(Intimate Moments #737, September 1996).

KATE
A job as a nanny leads her to Aaron Carver,
his adorable baby daughter and the
fulfillment of her dreams in KEEPING KATE
(Special Edition #1060, October 1996).

Meet these three siblings from

Silhouette SPECIAL EDITION®
and

INTIMATE MOMENTS®
™ *Silhouette*

REUNION

Continuing in October from Silhouette Books...

This exciting new cross-line continuity series unites five of your favorite authors as they weave five connected novels about love, marriage—and Daddy's unexpected need for a baby carriage!

You loved

THE BABY NOTION by Dixie Browning
(Desire 7/96)

BABY IN A BASKET by Helen R. Myers
(Romance 8/96)

MARRIED...WITH TWINS! by Jennifer Mikels
(Special Edition 9/96)

And the romance in New Hope, Texas, continues with:

HOW TO HOOK A HUSBAND (AND A BABY)
by Carolyn Zane (Yours Truly 10/96)

She vowed to get hitched by her thirtieth birthday. But plain-Jane Wendy Wilcox didn't have a clue how to catch herself a husband—until Travis, her sexy neighbor, offered to teach her what a man really wants in a wife....

And look for the thrilling conclusion to the series in:

DISCOVERED: DADDY
by Marilyn Pappano (Intimate Moments 11/96)

DADDY KNOWS LAST continues each month...
only in ▼ *Silhouette*®
TM

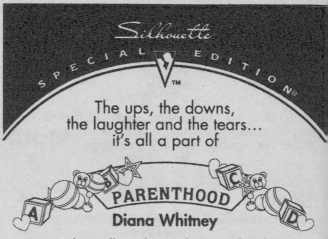

Silhouette

SPECIAL EDITION™

The ups, the downs,
the laughter and the tears...
it's all a part of

PARENTHOOD

Diana Whitney

Stories that will touch your heart and make you
believe in the power of romance and family. They'll
give you hope that true love really *does* conquer all.

DADDY OF THE HOUSE (SE #1052, September 1996)
tells the tale of an estranged husband and wife, who can't
seem to let go of the deep love they once shared...or
the three beautiful—and mischievous—children they
created together.

BAREFOOT BRIDE (SE #1073, December 1996)
explores the story of an amnesiac bride who is discovered
by a single dad and his two daughters. See how this
runaway rich girl becomes their nanny and then
their mother....

A HERO'S CHILD (coming March 1997)
reveals a husband who's presumed dead and comes home
to claim his wife—and the daughter he never knew he had.

You won't want to miss a single one of these delightful,
heartwarming stories. So pick up your copies soon—only
from Silhouette Special Edition.

"Just call me Dr. Mom....

I know everything there is to know about birthing
everyone else's babies. I'd love to have one of
my own, so I've taken on the job as nanny to three
motherless tots and their very sexy single dad,
Gib Harden. True, I'm no expert, and he's more
handy at changing diapers than I—but I have a
feeling that what this family really needs is the
tender loving care of someone like me...."

MOM FOR HIRE
by
Victoria Pade
(SE #1057)

In October, Silhouette Special Edition brings you

THAT'S MY BABY!
Sometimes bringing up baby can bring surprises...
and showers of love.

This October, be the first to read these wonderful authors as they make their dazzling debuts!

Women to Watch

THE WEDDING KISS by Robin Wells
(Silhouette Romance #1185)
A reluctant bachelor rescues the woman he loves from the man she's about to marry—and turns into a willing groom himself!

THE SEX TEST by Patty Salier
(Silhouette Desire #1032)
A pretty professor learns there's more to making love than meets the eye when she takes lessons from a sexy stranger.

IN A FAMILY WAY by Julia Mozingo
(Special Edition #1062)
A woman without a past finds shelter in the arms of a handsome rancher. Can she trust him to protect her unborn child?

UNDER COVER OF THE NIGHT by Roberta Tobeck
(Intimate Moments #744)
A rugged government agent encounters the woman he has always loved. But past secrets could threaten their future.

DATELESS IN DALLAS by Samantha Carter
(Yours Truly)
A hapless reporter investigates how to find the perfect mate—and winds up falling for her handsome rival!

Don't miss the brightest stars of tomorrow!

Only from ▼ *Silhouette*®
TM